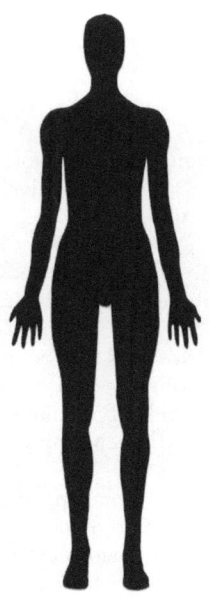

An A-Girl Studio book
published 2017 in the USA.

For additional information, please contact:
A-Girl Studio
P.O. Box 213, Burbank, CA 91503 U.S.A.
www.a-girlstudio.com

ISBN: 978-1-936622-38-2

First paperback edition, 2017

RAPACIOUS

By
Elizabeth Watasin

A-GIRL STUDIO

CHAPTER ONE

Nuit Four's vast interior slowly rotated above Kyn, ancient hieroglyphics spelled out in the shapes of the affluent station sectors. Sprawling silver habitats surrounded spots of greenery and blue water, and artificial sunlight glinted along Nuit's colossal ribs. Right then, the distant sun Merope shone outside the space station with the planet Darqueworld spinning at Nuit's orbital center. The smelly sector Kyn stood in was called the Pong, and there the illegal, the unlicensed, and the desperate operated.

Kyn licked an ice cream cone, her tongue slow and meditative. One hand pushed back her leather jacket to rest on her hip. Dark-haired and tall, her heavy-lidded and lazy gaze veiled her surveillance of the littered street, deserted except for herself and the ice cream seller whose cart carried more than ice cream. Of the Nuit space stations, Nuit Four was the shortest step a traveler could take away from Darquekind's homeworld for a nascent adventure into the galaxy. School children visited. Business people met, negotiated, and traded. Dreamers possessing nothing came and remained, stranded. And rogues set up their small schemes in the Pong, away from Darqueworld's unsparing eye.

A pale girl with white hair and smudged eyeliner crept across the street. Her still lungs and cold energy marked her as a vampire.

The ice cream seller hurried away, his cart's bell tinkling. Apparently, he did not think he had the recreational euphorics the vampire might want to buy.

The girl stopped near. Her gaze traveled from Kyn's boots to her long-legged, tight trousers, low-slung belt, black stretch-tee defining a muscled abdomen and small breasts, and then paused at her face. Wonderment entered her gaze at the red fire rimming Kyn's green irises. Kyn gazed sideways at the street and lazily licked her cone.

"Are you a rock star?" the vampire whispered. Her tongue moistened her lips.

Kyn brought her cone down.

Infant, she hand signed. *Be safe*.

The girl's cold eyes glinted. She might not know intragalactic sign language, but Kyn's communication intrigued.

"You're deaf?" Kyn shook her head. "Mute?" The girl stepped close. "How can you not have a voice? Darquekind can fix anything."

The corner of Kyn's mouth crept up. Children.

She brought up a hand in one half the gesture of prayer, touched her forehead, and then dropped her prayer hand down the center of her face.

Gods, she signed.

A skysyke rumbled above, shadowing the street and sending the girl's white locks and Kyn's dark mane flying. The tail of the departing vehicle bore corporate markings: Skycourt Industries

The vampire hissed. Kyn turned and scanned for what had upset her. The girl fled for the buildings' shadows.

In the littered street, a tall woman walked, her shining hair light and her skin dark golden. Her angled, silver eyes and the facial circuit traces beneath her skin caught the artificial sunlight, revealing her biomechanical nature. Anja—who was once Aine the Sixth, celestial Perfect and fallen servant of the divine holarchy—strolled.

Kyn's lip curled, heartbeat thundering.

Anja looked like she'd left a leather and mahogany furnished office to play in a ship's hangar, and then dropped from a skysyke to enjoy a walk in the Pong. She wore a tailored men's silk button down tucked into tailored black trousers. Her leather braces were tan. Sleeves neatly rolled to below her elbows, she hefted a cutting torch in one hand. A faceted wood fountain pen with silver trim sat clipped to a breast pocket.

Kyn recalled a diminished and disorientated Anja; her once blest state revoked after being cast out from the heavenly realm to impact Again NewYork. Though Skycourt Industries swiftly appropriated the former celestial scientist and contracted Kyn to protect her, it took a year for Anja to rebuild an identity. She had been—and still was—nothing like Aine the Fourth or Aine the Fifth, the Perfects Kyn had known.

Anja stopped before her, and Kyn's veiled gaze slid away, hiding flickering fire.

Discontentment and desire roiled. She should feign civility and peck Anja on the cheek as amiable ex-lovers did. Kiss her possessively; have her roughly in the street.

"Did I pull you away from your nest of women?" Anja said. Her free hand signed as well. She smirked slightly.

Kyn watched the street, choices warring.

"Please don't withdraw," Anja said, low.

Kyn thrust out her cone.

Anja brightened. Subcutaneous circuit lights danced briefly over one brow. She leaned in and licked the ice cream.

Six women, Kyn's other hand told her.

"That is many for you."

Perhaps it was. Each brief den Kyn made, she filled with sex companions, forming a warm-bodied, temporary pack around her.

Two were twins, she signed. She gave her cone to Anja.

From the corner of her eye, Kyn noticed the hidden vampire stir in the shadows.

"The Again Walker does not know what you are, as many don't." Anja bit the cone's rim.

Kyn shrugged, the barest lift of one shoulder. She could say the same of Anja. Kyn's true form was irresistible to dark Other-beings, unknowingly attracted by a whiff of hellfire. Anja's once-form usually made them run away—even if they had no clue why. She indicated the cutting torch Anja held.

"You told me to carry something when walking alone, and this was in my hand." Anja turned the ice cream cone at precise increments and crunched it until it was gone, then licked her thumb. "What is wrong?"

This was a bad idea, Kyn said. She turned to leave.

"I still need your help." Anja's quiet tone was urgent.

"You're Emissary Aine," the vampire suddenly interrupted, stepping near.

Kyn froze at the words.

"I am not," Anja said evenly. "Aine the Fifth is deceased, and I am Sixth."

"Then she did die and not disappear. Like Elvis. I guess you god-servants can do that. Die, I mean." The vampire held out her hands, palms open. "Alms," she demanded.

Before Anja could comply, fire flared in Kyn's eyes.

LEAVE. She stomped her foot at the vampire, who fled.

"Kyn," Anja said.

You're always in trouble. Kyn walked away.

"As you once said, I'm still a child."

Lights raced at Anja's temple. Then her chin lifted as if she'd confessed to nothing. With no memory of her celestial existence, she was—counting from her fall—barely two years old.

Then explain, Kyn demanded.

Anja's light-traces lessened. "As I told you in my message, my bio-dats were lifted during a security scan here on Nuit Four. The breach is under investigation."

Your dats, not parts of you, Kyn clarified.

"A biological sample? No. The exabytes of data stored in my DNA remain safe."

Anja's confidence—and teasing tone—irritated. The data the gods hid inside their Perfects was deeply encrypted, designed to corrupt once leaving Anja's body. But Kyn had been a thorough, if not paranoid, bodyguard where Anja was concerned. She hadn't even let Anja's sweat on a towel or her saliva on a drinking glass leave her protection. She gestured for Anja to continue.

"I've traced the sale of my body scan to there."

Anja motioned across the street. A two-story front with shielded windows sat, one lone door facing them. She pursed her full lips and silently whistled.

Kyn blocked her ears against the ultrasonic frequency. It triggered a disguised holo-sign: *FEMFLESH*

The animated neon figure beneath was of a well-endowed robotic female.

Kyn rolled her eyes and swept a V sign up. She briefly pressed the back of the sign to her forehead.

Stupid, her gesture said.

"The desire to profit from artificial sex slaves is revisited whenever chrono-immigrants arrive at Darqueworld," Anja said. "It is always a new idea to them."

Kyn repeated the hand sign. *Dumb. It's been done.* The bio-mechanical Artificials of Darquekind—who made up the Makepeace and the Janes—were the centuries old end product of human experimentation with synthetic beings. The Perfects were the same result for the gods.

Gods made A-s-p-a-r—Kyn could not recall the spelling.

"The Apsarasa, yes. I am certain I'm not of the host of celestial comfort companions." Anja's tone was light.

Kyn snorted. She'd never thought that. Anja the Sixth—like Aine the Fourth and Fifth before her, still possessed the height and impressive build of a Perfect of the Valkyrie, despite acting the celestial scientist she professed to be.

"Femflesh is an illegal venture," Anja continued. "The business partners are chrono-refugees from a technologically inferior era. When experimentation becomes a problem, Nuit Four authorities let it self-resolve in the Pong."

Kyn raised a brow. So much for the care and rights of new artificial life.

You're certain they have your dats? she asked.

Anja presented her palm.

Subdermal circuit lights darted beneath the hand's skin. A holo interface projected, bearing the logo of Femflesh.

Beneath the logo, a nude figure resembling Anja slowly spun. More windows displayed her breasts, buttocks, and—

A whispery sound emitted from Kyn's throat. She was laughing.

Anja's brow lifted. "Perhaps it is amusing. Especially if there is one in their database of you."

Why am I here? Kyn demanded.

"To help me destroy what they stole."

Advocate? Kyn said.

"As an illicit business, Femflesh has no fear of legal threat. But they can fear you."

That was true. Kyn had one more question.

Sky-court?

Anja's silver-eyed gaze dimmed.

"Nuit Four is my first move away from Darqueworld and Skycourt's guardianship, and already my personal security has been compromised. You warned me that independence would not be easy. You also said you believed I could succeed on my own.

"You are the only one who thinks so. I must resolve this myself." Anja's gaze held Kyn's. "You left me, but I trust you. And I cannot trust Skycourt."

Kyn turned for the building and motioned: *come.*

"Thank you." Anja's hand duplicated her gratitude. "We will have dinner after." Her tone held the quiet assurance of having the final word.

Kyn thrust her thumb to her chest, the fingers splayed.

Fine, her curt gesture said.

※

Anja placed her right hand on the door. The celestial

holarchy's sacred hieroglyph threaded beneath the skin of her hand's back, faintly glowing. Light brightened beneath her palm as she broke the door's pass codes.

"And you're on Nuit Four for what business?" Anja politely inquired.

Ambassador's daughter, Kyn said.

"To protect or seduce?" The door slid open.

Kyn grabbed the cutting torch from Anja's hand and left it by the door before they entered. The womb-like red of the shadowy corridor reminded her of shabby brothels.

"How long is the assignment for?" Anja was being uncharacteristically chatty. Kyn placed a hand at the small of Anja's back before she could prevent herself. Nose drifting near Anja's neck, she inhaled familiar fresh sweetness. Sharp yearning rose.

She recalled: Anja stumbling in a hospital gown, newly fallen and attempting words. Anja cool and collected, speaking science's dispassionate language, her tone colder than Aine-5's—more rational than Aine-4's. Anja, in her Skycourt-provided lab, focused and lost within invisible worlds.

Anja, who did not know why she fell, and who was becoming more and more the Perfect the gods might have mysteriously planned for—or weren't expecting.

Kyn turned her face away.

Why the torch? she asked instead.

"I am fixing a little ship." Anja's soft, pleased tone was one she used when happy about a project. "I will gift it to someone before leaving. And your assig—?"

Two weeks, Kyn brusquely gestured. *I'm escorting the daughter to Nuit Three.*

"I am going there as well," Anja said.

Kyn glanced at her sharply. When they stepped into the

red room at corridor's end, a holo program triggered.

Two more holos activated as Kyn and Anja crossed the small, sparse room for a counter with an interface surface, each projection playing the same round-faced fellow in scruffy beard and curly hair. A red curtain hung behind the counter.

"Femflesh, the only erotic tech you need," the holo-man said, "because simuladildonics? That's complicated. All you want is to do the deed, right here, right now, right? That's Femflesh: orifices, visual cues, and *flesh*."

When the holos winked out, Kyn shared a raised brow with Anja.

Anja touched the counter's interface. A large gallery of intimate female anatomy projected.

"Their selection of orifices," she noted. "This comprehensive variety of vulvas may be familiar to you."

Kyn pointed at one labeled *Angel*.

"It is interesting seeing mine next to others." Anja touched the interface again, summoning a gallery of breasts. "With this flesh technology you can make your perfect nest of women. She can have twenty breasts and ten vaginas."

I like REAL women, Kyn said. Since when did Anja have a problem with her sleeping preference? It had taken so many to fill the void left by Aine-4. Six last night to fill the emptiness left by Anja.

Thinking women, Kyn said, insistent.

Anja watched her surreptitiously. She never ignored Kyn during a conversation, but seemed reluctant right then to share her full gaze.

Real women smell good, taste good. Feel *good.* Kyn's hands glided. *Talk. Laugh. Get sad. Mad. Sometimes too much—*

"But enough for temporary company." Anja's hands spoke

too.

My den women, yeah, Kyn said.

"Perhaps I'm not so real. I cannot even be company for you. Was I not complicated enough?"

Kyn pulled Anja to face her.

Anja's breath rate was elevated, and her scent fleeting. Her silvered pupils were pinpoints. When Anja was very upset, her trace lights dulled, and Kyn remembered that their last fight had begun the same way.

You are very real, Kyn said.

"We shouldn't have parted."

You—are leaving—Darqueworld, Kyn slowly said. She looked into Anja's eyes until they calmed and dilated. *Becoming yourself. Our paths are diverging.*

"I *wanted* you to come with me." Anja's gestures softened with her gaze. "You, who also felt the need to leave. It is my fault I did not make that clear. But you will not travel with me. It seemed we mutually agreed. I am inadequate."

Kyn stilled Anja's hands. She'd never said that.

"I compete with ghosts. I will never be Aine-4 or 5." Anja's tone cracked slightly.

Stop, Kyn said. *You are the smartest. Most intelligent Aine. I'm the one i-n-a-d-e-qu—* she spelled, and Anja kissed her.

Their mouths warred. Anja held Kyn's face, and Kyn swept her up, lifting her. Anja's back landed on the counter.

Biomechanical beings were heavier than the average human. A crack sounded from the interface's surface.

WOOP, an alarm blared.

Kyn pulled herself off Anja, listening for clues that might have caused the alarm. She smelled no fire. The blaring then switched to a bell's sharp ringing. Beyond the room's entrance, the building's front door rumbled as a shield descended before it.

The shield landed with a boom, firmly engaging. The locking mechanism spun and then clicked.

"You should not have left my torch outside," Anja said.

The ringing bell cut as Kyn helped Anja off the table. Feet hurried down a corridor behind the curtains and a male's voice desperately cursed. A bearded and curly haired man emerged.

"*Whoa*," he yelled, and Kyn's fist stopped short of his face. She drew back, fist still hovering over the counter. "Customers! Okay! I'm Dirk Fisher." He offered his hand to Kyn, who merely glared, and then turned to Anja. "*Whoa* again. This just gets crazier. You look nice, though." He shook Anja's hand. "Nicer than, um—sorry about the lockdown! Building's—uh, it's still new to us! My associate hit the wrong button." He laughed, his eyes stark and wide. "Are you ladies here for some Femflesh quality time? You should come back later."

"We cannot leave," Anja said.

"You're right! And neither can I. What would you like to order?"

"You have flesh units on the premises for our...pleasure?" Anja said.

"Are you a cop?" Fisher said. "One of those...." He indicated his own brow while staring at the soft, subdermal lights at Anja's temple. "Makepeace? Because we can work something out."

Kyn pulled Anja back by the Y of her braces and leaned in. She winked.

"Oh yeah, we can do a 'try before you buy,'" Fisher said quickly. "In a couple of days? Or work on that custom flesh-morph for you. I'll even throw in some Rock Hard, female version. And if you want a stage two Femflesh doll with features and hair, that's extra." He paused, his stare suddenly stricken. Fisher cleared his throat. "We're, ah, we're having a two for one orifices special this week, but I'll make that three if you lady cops can help me out on something."

Kyn's gaze narrowed.

"I would like to know about her." Anja presented her palm and summoned the nude holo resembling herself. The holo-Anja slowly rotated.

"She's not available," Fisher said.

"Who helped you steal this bio-data?" Anja asked.

"I know what you want." Fisher pointed at Kyn. "Twins. Demon twins."

Kyn indicated the holo of nude Anja, then Anja herself.

"A Femflesh of her? Gotcha. Twins. Nice outfit you dressed her in, by the way. Really handsome."

Kyn slammed her palm on the counter, cracking it further. Fisher jumped.

"I am an individual, not a manufactured plaything," Anja said evenly. She ended the projection. "And you stole my bio-dats—"

"You're not a robot?" Fisher said.

"Along with those of other females," Anja finished.

"Any likenesses to people or life forms living, dead, celebrity, or fictional are purely accidental and unintentional and coincidental," Fisher said. His throat cleared again.

He darted for the curtains. Kyn hooked the back of his jacket's collar. Fisher shimmied out of the garment and fled.

Kyn jumped the counter and tore the curtains back just

as a shield door slid to shut. She braced her back against the doorframe, one hand holding the shield door open. Hydraulics screamed. Anja squeezed underneath Kyn's straining arm and stepped inside.

Kyn let go and followed Anja in, the door slamming shut behind them.

CHAPTER TWO

"We must locate their database," Anja said. Her silver eyes shone in the corridor's dim light. Doors led to shadowed rooms on either side, each marked *Parlor* with a number.

Kyn nodded, her scanning gaze shifting from the hall to Anja.

If there's a sex doll of you, what do you want done? she asked.

"Assuming it is capable of independent thought and action, I can send it to Skycourt Industries as my replacement," Anja said.

Kyn grinned.

"Since you prefer real women, I know not to give it to you," Anja then remarked. "Especially if you found it indistinguishable from me."

Kyn's grin disappeared, but for another reason. She'd been aware of a problem since dealing with the shield door, the rich metallic odor filling the hallway.

Don't look, she told Anja. She approached one of the doors and cautiously opened it.

Within, a man's fresh remains lay on the bed, his trousers

around the ankles. What remained of his pelvis was a pulped mess of flesh and blood, still bright red. He stared wide-eyed, the blue-lipped and bruised mouth stretched open.

Kyn scanned the ceiling, then the sides of the room beyond the doorframe. The blood-splattered killer had not left footprints.

She shut the door, brow darkened.

There's a murderer in the building, she said.

Anja considered her words. "I will alert Nuit." Her silver eyes flashed.

Lights chased briefly along her left temple. Frowning, she opened her palm and projected the station's hieroglyph. An error message superimposed.

"The building is more than shielded." Her gaze turned inward, studying internally received data. "Analysis of the signal bounces suggests jammers, activated throughout the building...yet for what purpose?"

Kyn rubbed her lip. She glanced sideways at the shield door.

"My data," Anja reminded.

Fine, Kyn said and moved down the corridor. She then swiveled and snapped two fingers tips down on the pad of her thumb at Anja: *NO.*

Anja coolly lifted her hand from the door leading into the dead man's room and followed.

"How did the victim die?" Anja asked, her tone low as Kyn focused on the corridor's end. Curtains covered the exit.

No talking, Kyn said curtly.

You looked at the ceiling. Then you wanted to leave. Anja's hands spoke within Kyn's peripheral vision.

Is the murderer another Other-being? Anja's hands continued. *A succubus? A—*

QUIET, Kyn said. The scent of more spilled blood lay beyond the curtain. Kyn stood aside and cautiously pulled the fabric back.

Anja walked through it.

What—the HELL, Kyn said, throwing up her hands. She followed, stepping on to a broad stairwell landing. A door sat ajar beside the foot of the stairs leading up. Anja walked across and stopped before the dead man by the door, his back slumped against the wall and his trousers around his ankles. He'd died in the same manner as the other dead man.

"Brutal," Anja said, pensive.

Kyn glanced through the open doorway and noted the office furniture. She recalled Fisher's words.

Who are the partners? she asked.

Anja summoned her palm's holo interface. Photos of the three Femflesh owners displayed: Dirk Fisher, Kip Araras, and Ben Harriman.

Kip Araras lay dead before them.

Kyn shrugged out of her leather jacket. She held it open for Anja. Once Anja slipped into it, Kyn moved for the office's doorway. The bones of her flexing hand audibly cracked as her nails extended, sharp-pointed. Her shoulders, chest, and back broadened, and the fiery flicker of her irises grew.

She cautiously entered and approached the holo table. The archaic, biometric padlock secured over the tabletop's holo interface prompted a brief eye roll. When she looked at the locked holo projection, it flashed red for the lockdown. A handheld pad-shaped device—an Id—lay face down on the floor. Kyn picked it up, its screen cracked.

"Baby, he didn't just take my bio-dats, he took a *sample* of me," a young woman's recording said as the holo came to life. Her Afro was dyed purple. "Just dump the creep, already."

The holo glitched. "Just dump the creep, already," the woman repeated.

Kyn laid the Id facedown on the table. Except for an over-turned chair, the office appeared undisturbed. Kip Araras had been attacked upon leaving. A glance into the darkened walk-in closet confirmed a few stored boxes, nothing more. She left the closet doors open and returned to the room's entrance.

"Someone copulated with Araras hard enough to pulverize his pelvis," Anja pondered, "and extract his penis." Kneeling, Anja shut his eyes, and Kyn noticed the whites, riddled with broken blood capillaries. "But he may have died from being violently smothered…with something heavily lubricated."

Kyn put a curled thumb and forefinger in her mouth and whistled. She pointed at the holo table.

Anja entered and picked up the Id. The damaged holo message played.

"His sister?" she said. Kyn widened her eyes at her and pointed at the table again.

The middle finger of Anja's right hand clicked and split, extending a miniscule tool. She applied it to the padlock, and a tiny whirling sounded.

Kyn watched, grim. When Anja impacted Again New York, she had lacked a right forearm that was never found and which never regenerated. Kyn was still perturbed by Sky-court's gift of an Artificial's forearm. Though it functioned seamlessly with Anja's own biomechanical body and grafted skin, its servo-bot capabilities were glaringly crude for a Per-fect.

Anja's face held serenity. Tinkering gave her pleasure. As far as Kyn knew, both Anja and Skycourt still didn't know her scientific purpose, despite the tests and assignments given to her. Anja swiftly rendered the padlock into pieces.

Activating the holo table, she searched its contents. Kyn looked over Anja's shoulder.

"This workstation is for business management and accounting, nothing more. What would you like for dinner?"

Kyn froze. Anja had one thing in common with Aine-5; she knew how to sear steaks rare. Their dinners always led to more.

Kyn started to gesture.

"Dinner is not a bad idea," Anja countered while perusing the holo screen. "If your leaving is not about the Aines you loved before, then tell me why."

I told you, Kyn said, anger pricking.

"Tell me again." Anja turned to her, and Kyn's gaze fell to Anja's mouth.

Something dropped in the closet.

Kyn swiveled.

A female humanoid crouched, featureless except for its large lips. Iridescent and plum-colored, the skin shimmered as the body swayed on highly arched feet shaped into hooves. A jet-black ponytail cascaded down from atop the creature's head.

The creature rose, big breasts gleaming. Its prominent genitalia were bright pink.

Kyn kicked a chair, hurtling it in the creature's direction. It leapt, its vulva mimicking its wetly sucking mouth. It landed with a loud *clop* of its hooves and rushed forward. Kyn flipped up another chair and thrust it with one hand.

Plum flesh impacted the chair legs and crinkled like

inflated rubber. The creature's pelvis wildly pumped for Kyn's crotch. Lips smacked as the wet mouth strained for Kyn's own lips. Lubricant splattered Kyn's face.

The—FUCK, Kyn gestured.

"A basic flesh construct." Anja studied the creature. "Femflesh's fleshmorph. It is single-minded...obeying a simple directive."

To KILL us, Kyn answered. She shoved, sending the fleshmorph stumbling back. It surged, rounding to nearly grab Kyn as she blocked it again.

She allowed the fleshmorph to drive her back in a circle, Anja stepping out of the way. Hauling up the chair she'd kicked, Kyn walloped the creature.

It staggered, and Kyn swung again, shattering the chair. The fleshmorph's knees gave way. With a hard thrust, Kyn hurtled it back into the closet. She slammed it shut.

THUMP

The creature threw itself at the doors. Kyn jammed a chair's leg through the handles.

"Rapacious," Anja said as Kyn wiped her face.

NIGHTMARE, Kyn said.

Anja's lips quirked. "You are born of the guardians of below. How is its appearance worse than demons?"

My family guards the gates, I never ran around behind them. The closet thumped as Kyn pointed to the holo table.

"You want me to break the lockdown code now?" Anja's tone was uncertain.

This is the Pong. The police may be slow. But I don't want to stay longer and deal with this mess.

The closet continued to thump.

"The fleshmorph is as described." Anja hesitated by the table. "Orifices and visual cues."

Kyn motioned, *and?*

"It is something simply to 'do' and not think about. A basic design, but an error has been written. Perhaps that flesh-morph is not the only one gone amok."

This tech had its history of mistakes already. The sex doll of you may be another nightmare. I don't want to see it. Kyn's gaze slid away.

I don't want to take care of it, was what she'd really wanted to say.

"I understand," Anja said.

Kyn stood, hands on her hips.

"There's still the matter of my—"

DATA, fine, Kyn said.

Releasing the building from lockdown might allow a flesh-morph to escape. Kyn did not relish securing the creatures while Anja searched for her data. She didn't believe she could without destroying a few.

"What is it?" Anja asked as they departed the office.

I am not an exterminator. Kyn spelled the word. *This is not hunting.*

"I understand," Anja repeated, solemn. "Hunting is skill and respect for the hunted." She smiled. "Was not Aine the Fourth your most glorious quarry?"

The smile that broke on Kyn's face shone like her beloved Aine-4's own shining presence.

The hunt was so long, so wily. She killed all who came for her but me, she enthused. Kyn had never witnessed so singular a warrior. One who'd defied the gods and her sacred duty for higher purpose—one who'd earned the gods' death judgment that drew every hunter. Kyn's heart had been enslaved the moment she'd been given the scent of Aine the Fourth.

Anja touched her face.

"Hound," she whispered.

A sharp thump sounded from the office.

Anja's hand dropped, and a door clicked open in the landing above.

Kyn leapt up the stairs, nostrils flaring. She closed her hand around the cylinder of Fisher's archaic projectile weapon—a .38 special—and trapped it from firing. Fisher fell back.

"I was coming back to get you gals!" Fisher squeaked. "On second thought, I'd thought: I should let you Amazons in." He laughed weakly. "And here you are."

We are NOT A-m-a-z—

Anja stilled Kyn's spelling hand and helped Fisher up.

"Compared to Kyn's kindred, we are hardly Amazonian," she said.

Are those things up there? Kyn waved above.

"Are you asking if any—? Right! There's nobody!" Fisher said. "The second floor is shut for remodeling. No one's present."

Kyn pointed below. The trapped fleshmorph thumped against the closet.

"Well, okay, that. Our basic fleshmorphs respond to aroused people," Fisher said nervously. "They're programmed to want us when we're excited."

"Are they programmed to be violent about it?" Anja asked.

"No! I don't even know how—I can't...." Fisher waved the gun. "They're not even supposed to run around like that! They just went crazy."

"Then there are more. What is their usual behavior?" Anja asked.

"*Behavior*?" Fisher shrugged. "Besides…lying back and thinking of England?"

What, Kyn said.

Fisher hurriedly pointed above. "I was hoping to get out by the roof. To get help! Maybe you gals can try."

"Not yet. Take us to your database," Anja said.

"Sure! Ben, our genetics programmer, didn't know what went wrong, but maybe you can." Fisher led the way downstairs and looked up at Anja. "You look brainy."

"Thank you."

When they passed Kip's body on the main landing, Fisher averted his gaze, his wide eyes suddenly bleak.

"Darquekind is so amazing." He cleared his throat. "Full of Amazons. I should call Kip's, um—can one of you call out for me? My Id's communicator hasn't worked even before all hell broke loose—"

Kyn leapt past him as a curvaceous fleshmorph with a blonde ponytail stamped up the stairs, wet lips working in its featureless face.

Anja snatched Fisher back. The fleshmorph slammed into Kyn and grabbed her belt, its pelvis wildly thrusting against her. Its watermelon breasts smacked Kyn in the chin. Sucking lips descended for Kyn's mouth.

Anja grabbed the fleshmorph's ponytail and pulled.

Kyn took hold of the creature's arms and wrenched its grip off her hips. Fire erupted in her eyes, and her fangs emerged. Kyn's chest vibrated with a silent roar as her spine elongated. Vascular arms and chest expanded. She sank claws into the fleshmorph's back.

She flung both arms backwards and ripped the fleshmorph's body in two.

White blood splashed the landing, and stringy trails of

flesh whipped. The hoof-foot of the fleshmorph's headless half kicked Kyn in the crotch.

Stars exploded behind Kyn's eyes as the two fleshmorph halves wrested from her grasp. Her size diminished. She slipped in the creature's fluids and slammed her palms down on the landing. The halves tumbled down the stairs and dragged themselves across the lower landing and out of sight. The sliding of their wet flesh echoed in the stairwell and faded.

"Tearing it apart was extreme."

Kyn blinked the last stars away and glared at Anja, who knelt beside her.

Anja bit her lip and pulled back the hand she'd offered.

Kyn waved at the blood-smeared stairs. *HOW*, she demanded.

"I am not a bio-geneticist, Kyn, I don't know how it survived splitting in half," Anja answered evenly. They both looked at Fisher.

"I didn't know it could even do that," he said.

Kyn gingerly regained her feet. She adjusted her trousers, wincing.

"Do you need an ice pack?" Anja asked. She smirked slightly.

Kyn stilled. The quip reminded of a raw, consummate night. She and Anja had fought, and then made more than love. Kyn had clawed Anja's body.

Anja's smirk disappeared as if she remembered the same. She quickly looked away.

"I—I really liked how your tee shirt just *streeetched* to accommodate your bigger—" Fisher motioned across his chest.

"Kyn's breasts do not retain fatty tissue in her more muscular form," Anja remarked.

"I meant her pecs! Her pecs! Very Arnold. In the movies, that tee shirt would have been—" he gave a long whistle, imitating the sound of a bomb dropping. "Totally shredded. Did your leather pants do the same thing? Because that's really conven—"

Kyn snatched Fisher up by his button down's nape and marched him down the stairs.

CHAPTER THREE

The Femflesh laboratory, Fisher told them, was in the basement floor.

"Down here's where all the Femflesh magic happens."

They traversed a maintenance corridor, following the blood trail left by the ripped fleshmorphs. Pipes snaked above. The floor's intermittent grates revealed bio-waste convertors humming below, processing discarded lab matter to be recycled by Nuit.

While Fisher delivered a spiel about Femflesh, Kyn touched Anja, wanting her to meet her gaze. The night she'd raked Anja's back, she'd said many things; *I'm sorry. I love you. I love you so much.*

Joy had lit Anja's eyes to sun-rising intensity.

"You confuse me," Anja murmured. She refused to look at Kyn.

Kyn shut her eyes. Anja could have easily said, "hurt" instead.

I'm sorry. She hoped Anja watched from her peripheral vision.

Anja nodded.

"We partners had been buddies since college," Fisher continued. "Kip was the infrastructure, he knew how to put it together and run it. Maybe that's why he always got the girl. But between you and me...." Fisher leaned in confidence towards Anja. "Ben and I never had a chance with the girl. Especially Ben. Are you sure your Ids can't call out?"

Kyn sniffed. The scent of a fleshmorph intensified, and she jogged ahead.

"Your lockdown has blocked communication channels," Anja answered.

"Uh, okay. That's weird. Anyway, Ben's the tech stuff. Whatever our product was, he could make it reality. And I'm the face. I know how to market and bring in the money. Aw, geez." He rubbed his eyes. "His fiancée is going to—Kip is really gone."

"Does his fiancée have purple hair?"

"Yeah, now she does."

"What happened here?" Anja asked. "What went wrong?"

"Off the record?" Fisher sniffled and wiped his nose. "It's crazy, but all our basic fleshmorphs flipped out and made a break for it. One moment we're arguing with your—we were arguing, and the next thing, fleshmorphs were popping out of their juice stations and going crazy."

"You were arguing with who?" Anja said.

"So they ran," Fisher hurriedly continued. "All of them. Even the unfinished ones." He glanced ahead to Kyn, who waited for them at the corridor's junction. "There's a customer, by the way, who's going to be really unhappy you ripped up his custom Femflesh, Hildy Bottom."

Kyn's brow rose. She reached down into the adjacent corridor and brought up a blonde ponytail dangling a head and the ragged strips of a body.

"Cartilaginous." Anja cocked her head at the remains. "With a fluidic processing network. But not sophisticated enough to initiate self-repair. How do we destroy the flesh-morph's seat of mental process?"

"Uh," Fisher said, staring at the head Kyn held up.

"Kyn please put that away." Anja regarded Fisher. "They must have a mental command center."

Fisher nervously laughed. "Our basic fleshmorphs don't think. They're like bicycles, you ride—"

Kyn grabbed Fisher's collar front and twisted it.

"Sorry, sorry," he said hoarsely.

"Your flesh units do think," Anja said as Kyn held Fisher and pointed down the connecting corridor. "They know to hide, and they know to wait."

"Yes, the lab is that way," Fisher gasped. Kyn let his twisted collar go, his sneakers striking the floor. Fisher coughed.

"And they know to retreat," Anja said. She stood beside Kyn as they both regarded the new passageway. At the cor-ridor's end, the shadows of ponytailed heads traveled across the wall and disappeared.

When Kyn loped ahead for the retreating fleshmorphs, she found no trace of them in the long corridor that ran alongside hidden power generators. The walls provided little soundproofing; she could not detect movement beneath the low and furious rumble of the engines.

Nor could her nose track the creatures. Their manufactur-ing process had spread their synthetic scent everywhere, like rubber balls hiding in a rubber factory. Kyn inhaled for Anja, seeking contrast. Perfects and Artificials possessed individual scent signatures. She'd never been so comforted by that fact until right then.

She paused, marking Anja closer than where she'd left her. A glance down the way she'd come did not reveal a contrary Perfect following.

Kyn was surprised Anja wasn't already by her side, poised with an annoying question. The scent retreated. Kyn mentally shrugged and opened a floor grate's hatch doors. Thrusting her upper body into the opening, she scrutinized the darkness and bio-waste machinery.

She waited and listened, her night vision hunting the dark. Nothing attempted to attack. Kyn pulled herself out and shut the grating.

At the corridor's end, she peeked around the corner. The darkened passageway ahead terminated at shut doors with hazard signs lit by a lone light: the lab. Fleshmorphs of different female shapes and colors climbed and rubbed against the shut entrance. A fleshmorph made up of only purple-netted buttocks, pelvis, and long legs pranced back and forth before the doors with mincing steps.

Kyn returned to where Anja and Fisher waited by Hildy's remains.

"How are your fleshmorphs deactivated?" Anja said to Fisher.

"Like an off switch? I don't know if Ben planned one of those." Fisher waved his pistol. "We could shoot them in the head, maybe? That's what they do in the movies."

"A partial fleshmorph possessing no head still kicked Kyn in the groin," Anja said. Fisher giggled nervously.

Kyn stopped behind Fisher, and Anja reached for her. She gently picked something off Kyn's black tee: a long, blonde hair.

Kyn forgot to chastise her about following and scowled. Anja flicked the hair away.

How can people respond to these things? Kyn indicated Hildy and smacked the back of Fisher's head.

"Ow," Fisher said.

"It does possess enhanced visual cues." Anja's eyes lit, amused, and her hands also spoke. "Don't those arouse you?"

Do they arouse you? Kyn retorted.

"When the first synthetic beings were made, solely for sex, they became a fetish," Anja remarked thoughtfully.

"You mean the sexodus?" Fisher said.

"If it was called that during your chrono-period, then yes. Synthetic beings triggered the first sexual response of many young humans, becoming their only source of arousal or sexual fantasy." Anja's smile seemed self-deprecating. "Where do I fall in the arousal cycle?"

You were supposed to say I arouse you, Kyn said.

She instantly regretted her quip, but Anja's smile warmed, lights chasing briefly above her brow. Kyn never ceased to marvel at their darting playfulness, so unlike the crown-like brilliance that had graced Aine the Fourth's forehead or the serene, hearth glow at Aine-5's temple.

"You're the ultimate fantasy," Fisher said thoughtfully. "When your bio-dats showed up, we thought you were too good to be true."

"Then you *have* made a Femflesh copy of me." Anja's good humor dimmed.

Fisher took a breath. "Yes—okay, yes. But—I don't know how Ben did it, but your duplicate's so authentic. Like a real woman," he said hurriedly. "Talks, thinks, and—she's practically the difference between women and things."

"Dirk Fisher, she should have never begun as a thing."
Fisher stared at Anja and fidgeted. He turned to Kyn.
"Go ahead and smack me," he said.

Fisher confirmed that the lab lay beyond the generators.
He had no idea how many fleshmorphs lurked.

"Seven, I think. But you got two, right? Or maybe there's
twelve—uh, or twenty, including the ones that are only pel-
vises and legs. What did I *say*?" Fisher held his head as Kyn
raised her hand at him.

Kyn told Anja to take Fisher back to the ground floor's
office. Anja could then lift the lockdown once Kyn accessed
the lab and returned.

I will wipe your data for you, she promised.

"I need to see this doll of me," Anja insisted.

"I need to see what inventory survi—I need to see if Ben
is okay," Fisher said.

Kyn looked at him.

"You are so good at this sign language stuff," he said.

Ambush waiting, Kyn told Anja. *I did not see twenty.*

"Can you clear them away now so that we may pass?" Anja
requested.

FINE, Kyn said.

Fisher cocked his gun.

Do NOT shoot us, Kyn ordered.

"Gotcha. Anything that moves," Fisher replied.

They walked to the passageway, the unseen generators
rumbling. When they turned the corner, fleshmorphs waited.

Candy pink, bright latex red, grape, and shiny licorice black;
they hovered far down the corridor. One with a gymnast's

compact body dropped to its hands and arced hoofed feet over its body to touch its head. Another gracefully pirouetted, revealing a face and well-endowed torso gracing both back and front. Next to it, a fleshmorph giantess with two sets of legs and breasts swayed and trembled as if in anticipation.

Kyn moved down the corridor. Fire ignited in her eyes, and her chest and muscles grew.

Fisher stood before Anja, gun gripped in both hands and his feet antsy as Kyn's back broadened, her spine arching and her fingernails elongating into claws.

"Wolf hide, wolf hide," he chanted. "Yes!" He shook his fist when Kyn's hackles rose.

"Do you know how to use your weapon?" Anja asked.

"Sure, I've watched movies."

Anja waited until Kyn was a third of the way down the corridor, then followed.

"Hey!" Fisher scurried after.

The fleshmorphs backed away, leading Kyn down the passageway. She advanced swiftly, smelling nothing but synthetic skin and lubricated slickness. The echo of lips and other orifices wetly smacking intensified.

She targeted the giantess with four breasts and swiped, removing its head. The fleshmorph jumped, wrapping its four legs around Kyn's waist. As Kyn staggered, it squeezed together one set of breasts and sprayed milk in Kyn's face.

Kyn wiped her eyes in time to see the gymnastic flesh-morph bound high over the headless one. Thighs spread, it aimed its crotch.

Anja called. "Try to find their command center."

Kyn's head snapped back at impact and she fell, slamming into the ground. Both fleshmorphs energetically pounded her into the floor.

"*Gah*," Fisher yelled and fired three rounds, puncturing the fleshmorphs humping Kyn. Anja grabbed his nape.

Her ocular-targeting swiftly mapped a trajectory. She tossed him three feet up and five feet away as she kicked the torso-less fleshmorph that pranced swiftly for where he once stood. Her calculation sent it hurtling into the creature smothering Kyn's face. Fisher landed a half second sooner than her data's projection and stumbled. He pointed his gun at a pink fleshmorph diving down. It slid on its belly with its sucking mouth headed for his groin. Anja snatched him up again, Fisher wildly firing. She kicked the pink fleshmorph aside at a thirty-degree angle, bouncing it off the passage-way's wall.

"*Whoo hooo*," Fisher shouted, regaining his feet. "I'm in a Hong Kong movie—"

Anja tossed him again and booted a lime green fleshmorph into the ceiling pipes, the impact ringing a low-pitched key of D. Fisher sailed through the air.

The fleshmorph on Kyn's face rocked back from a

collision, allowing Kyn to gasp for air. She gripped its thighs and heaved, flinging it backwards into the four-breasted one straddling her. Sitting up and then pulling herself from under them, Kyn pinned them both to the ground and formed a knife-hand with rigid fingers and palm. She struck.

Her knife-hand punctured both bodies and struck ground. A fleshmorph jumped on her neck and wrapped its legs. Kyn pulled her arm out of sucking synthetic flesh. A fourth ran up, its pelvis headed for her face.

She grabbed the leg wrapped around her neck and wrenched it from its knee socket.

Anja yanked Fisher to her as a partial leg flew by. The creatures piled onto Kyn, flattening her. She heaved, dislodging fleshmorphs. Her teeth and claws tore away the ones that clung.

Her body whipped. Synthetic flesh ripped and splattered. Body parts spun. Fisher ducked.

"Good thing we're insured," he said weakly.

Anja moved him back, her ocular mapping pinpointing a safe radius from the white blood spray. She then visually recorded Kyn's savagery for analysis later. Such ferocity fascinated when it was not about sex.

Stop thinking, Kyn had admonished once during a playful tussle. *You know how to fight.*

I am not Aine the Fourth, Anja had said.

The stricken paling of Kyn's eyes at her words should not have surprised her. Kyn never wrestled with her again.

The candy pink fleshmorph latched vise-like legs around Kyn's waist and smothered her face in its breasts. Kyn staggered and sank claws into the creature's back.

Her shoulder blades contracted. Fluids burst from the creature's shredded flesh as Kyn's arms swung apart.

"This bloodbath is nastier than any anime," Fisher said, "yet I can't look away."

Anja left him to approach Kyn.

A flying breast smacked Fisher in the face.

SPLACK

The pink head of a fleshmorph wetly impacted the wall. It slid down, its drenched ponytail leaving a white smear.

Anja entered Kyn's line of sight, her attention on the ground while Kyn pried herself out of vise-like pink legs. Limbs tossed, Kyn then breathed, realizing all the flesh-morphs lay dismembered.

Fire ebbed in her eyes. Kyn slowly diminished, fangs and claws disappearing and her chest silently rumbling. She wiped at the synthetic blood, lubricant, and muck on her face.

When she flicked her hand, Anja moved an increment away, the gore landing without a drop touching her. Kyn's leather jacket remained pristine.

PAY ATTENTION, Kyn had violently motioned once when Anja wandered through pulse fire like a spectator. Precision was a Perfect's gift, but Aine-4 and 5 had never exhibited Anja's flagrant disregard for personal safety, as if she were too enrapt in the invisible, ocular data her eyes processed to care.

I see as thou sees, Aine the Fourth had once explained, *but with shields of light before me, spinning words and measures.*

Projected holo disks; circular interfaces. Anja had shown

Kyn how Perfects saw by demonstrating with a holo animation. She liked analyzing Kyn down to the minute measures
of her breath, body heat, and body surfaces…when Anja
verbalized such intimacies, Kyn always needed to seduce her
right then.

A fleshmorph's hand flopped towards Anja, who knelt to
inspect shredded muscle fibers. Kyn stomped on it.

"We *rock*," Fisher shouted and played air guitar.

Kyn huffed, smelling nothing but synthetic flesh even with
Anja near. She cleared each nostril with a farmer's blow and
then spat. Fisher jumped before the glob could hit his shoes.

"Hey, um, when you did your werewolf thing, did I see you
grow…*horns*?" He made "horn" signs at his temples. "Because that means you're not a werewolf."

"She is a hellhound," Anja murmured.

Breasts wiggled on the floor. Kyn ignored them and focused on Anja tossing her shining hair aside. Anja then
poked her fountain pen's etched nib within a fleshmorph's
burst head.

"There is no brain," Anja noted.

She moved on to a torn open torso and crouched before
it to inspect its interior. Kyn admired the shape of Anja's
ass and kicked at the bulbous buttocks with legs, still crawl-
ing. She'd had enough of replicated flesh. If anyone were to
hand her a simulated vulva right then, she'd make that person
eat it.

But I am synthetic too, she imagined Anja saying.

When Anja straightened, studying something in her palm,
Kyn stepped near. She slowly ran her forefinger down Anja's
firm belly.

What were rubber balls compared to Perfects? Kyn would
need to strongly fantasize desire for a fleshmorph, and that

skill wasn't her strength. There was power and joy in seducing intelligence. Women were unpredictable, fascinating. Utter bitches at times, but when things were good—when Anja loved, she made sex—

Beautiful and messy.

"Kyn?" Anja asked. She might have said something Kyn had missed.

Kyn's lip lifted in a leer. She stuck her tongue out and made the slow motion of two women together: *sex.*

Anja glanced at the jiggling breasts.

"Is the aftermath of carnage arousing you?" she quietly asked.

No. She loved it when Anja became tousled and mindless. Voracious. Anja's fall had left her in fragments, emitting primal utterances in the celestial tongue. Then neurogenesis took effect; intellect asserted and internal order ruled. But when against Kyn's skin and digging into her flesh, Anja was—

Anja's silvered pupils slowly dilated as Kyn's hands moved. *Never doubt how real you are. Joyful, lustful. Loving. You; needful. You; giving. You are more than* good *sex.*

Lights shone above Anja's brow.

"I am that because of you," she said softly.

"Gals, gals." Fisher squeezed between their bodies and faced them. "Wow." He looked at his blood-smeared sleeve. "You need a shower. Gals, I am really enjoying our camaraderie here. We make a great team, don't you think? Brains, brawn, and me, business."

"Business?" Anja smiled. "What of your remaining partner, Ben Harriman?"

"Ben is great, but between you and me?" Fisher lowered his voice. "He can be, uh, anti-social? And now that we've arrived at Darqueworld, the flesh-tech is making him nigh intolerable. Just keep that in mind. I think he's a little afraid of alpha women." Fisher leaned back. "But hey, you—and you—and me? Potential! You need a manager. And one who totally gets you." He held up his Id. "I even put intragalactic sign language on my Id," he said, gleefully.

Kyn rolled her eyes and walked away. The lab and this weird Ben waited.

"Even without translation, I still understood what you just signed with your tongue to Ms. Perfect, here." Fisher turned to Anja and loudly whispered. "But I've been wondering. How come she hasn't gotten a new...." He pointed to his throat.

"Gods," Anja answered. Her single prayer hand touched her forehead in gentle reverence and moved down the center of her face.

"Riight." He duplicated the gesture. "Gods. Hey, say something to me!" he called to Kyn. "I'll sign back. Hold on." He paused and pecked at his Id.

Arms burst through the doors of the floor grate behind him and grabbed his legs. They dragged Fisher swiftly into the opening.

"FUCK NOOO—" Fisher screamed, clawing. His chest abruptly stuck fast in the grate.

Anja grabbed him beneath the armpits as Fisher jerked violently. She pulled up.

A ragged, wet rip sounded, and Fisher convulsed.

Drips struck the metal surface below him.

He slumped, a sack Anja hugged as his life's light faded.

✺

Kyn dove through another grate when Anja attempted to pull Fisher up. She fell upon the fleshmorphs below who'd torn him in half, his blood splattering along with theirs.

When she quickly returned to the passageway, Anja still held him.

"Vahalla," she whispered.

Kyn knelt. She pressed her head against Anja's.

A brave death, Kyn gently gave. She repeated the words when she unfolded Anja's arms from Fisher's body.

CHAPTER FOUR

Fisher had said twenty fleshmorphs might be lurking, but that was not how many Kyn had dismembered.

Four more tried to drag her into the maintenance tunnel as Anja stood before the lab doors, breaking its access password. She waited for Kyn to rejoin her.

The large room they slipped into was devoid of presence. While Anja re-secured the entrance, Kyn quickly prowled, the sticky soles of her boots squelching. Life-sized glass canisters sat tilted up in rows, open and empty. Juice stations; the rejuvenators Makepeace and Janes utilized. Perfects also benefited from such beds, but Anja had long weaned herself from a special rejuvenator Skycourt built when she first fell to Darqueworld, one that had fed Anja the power of the sun.

"The fleshmorphs can't sustain their energetic need to copulate for long," Anja murmured, and fell silent.

She hugged herself in Kyn's jacket. When she approached a workstation with glossy paper decorating its walls, Kyn trailed after. Kyn recognized the taped up and pinned ritual. Paper dependent chrono-immigrants liked to tear images out of archaic print magazines and display them. Blonde women filled one wall section; women with eyes angled like Anja's, another. Each picture grouping seemed to focus on a physical trait.

Anja glanced half-heartedly at a wall of beautiful, dark-haired women, and then summoned the workstation's interface. Kyn tapped at the unresponsive control panel of the lab's inner doors.

She motioned for Anja, who stared sightlessly at the workstation's holo screen, her hands still.

The pose prompted a memory; Aine-5, dressed in silk and decorated with medals in her darkened suite on Nuit Six, mourning her beloved cat.

Gel tubes lay in a pile on a medical tray. Kyn picked one up: *Rock Hard for Women.* Walking over to Anja, she lingered, aware of her own mucked state. She slipped the tube into her jacket's inner breast pocket.

Anja's brow circuits briefly lit beneath a smear of white blood. Her hands then glowed within the holo interface as she began breaking access codes. Kyn stared at the synthetic bloodstain marring Anja's face that the press of her own forehead might have placed there.

Another memory returned, unbidden; Aine the Fourth, her armor breached and her shining blood lifting in a desolate planet's air.

An anguished howl welled within Kyn, ascending.

Anja touched Kyn's face.

Her four fingers gently pressed. Kyn turned to inhale from Anja's glowing palm.

"I'm searching for a procedure giving the fleshmorphs a seat of mental process." Anja's tone was solemn. Her hand fell away. "Especially to experience pleasure—the simulated release of oxytocin and other chemicals."

Why? Kyn softly asked. She didn't think sex used violently had anything to do with pleasure.

"The presence of this research in Ben Harriman's personal folders." Anja paused the holo data at one page. "It discusses stimulating hyper-sexuality in the limbic regions of the brain. Not only do the fleshmorphs have no brain to stimulate, they cannot receive the reward due a hyper libido. They are simply driven to mimic copulation."

What about their thinking? Kyn said. *The luring. The ambush?*

Anja pulled her fountain pen from her breast pocket and uncapped it. She tapped the cap into her palm. A tiny processing wafer fell out and twinkled. "I retrieved this from one of the remains. It is highly antiquated but adequate for programming basic actions and reactions executed by the flesh unit's fluidic network, nothing more. There is no data here addressing the issue of independent thought...or solving it. It seems Fisher was right."

Anja paused, as if debating further words. She returned to the holo screen. "I think you should find Ben Harriman."

Kyn's gaze darkened at Anja's unspoken suspicion.

Anja held her lit palm to the holo screen, changing it to the image of the rotating nude Anja. It blipped to black, deleted, and scores of data flashed, rapidly erasing.

Kyn returned to the lab's internal doors and ripped the access panel away, then reconsidered rewiring the doors open. If fleshmorphs waited on the other side, she wanted the doors able to shut.

I need you, Kyn said, rejoining Anja. Anja stared wide-eyed at the holo screen.

Kyn peered as the data winked out.

Hydraulics hissed. The inner doors slowly opened.

Kyn moved before Anja. Within the widening opening, five women stood.

Lips glossed, cheekbones blushed, and fingernails painted, their willowy bodies were draped in long, sleeveless pastel colored gowns. Glittering paste jewelry dangled from their ears and adorned their wrists and bosoms. They held up brightly colored pistols and stared, unfocused and inscrutable.

A blonde, a redhead, a woman with hair of midnight—Kyn approached a brunette. Her perfume barely masked her synthetic scent, and her large brown eyes held no recognition. The pistol in her hand was a plastic toy.

"You two," a male voice called, sharp and quavering. "Stay where you are."

Kyn's lip lifted, snarling. She pushed by the Femflesh dolls. A skinny man with a crooked haircut and black-rimmed glasses nervously watched from behind an empty rejuvenator. A sniff told Kyn Ben Harriman was the lone human presence in the lab.

"S-stay back," he squeaked.

Kyn rushed for him, teeth bared.

No defensive weaponry materialized, and the dolls did not react. Ben screamed as Kyn hauled him up by his shirt's front and dropped him inside the rejuvenator. She shut the glass casing and locked it. Ben's yells emitted, muffled, as he pounded dully on the glass.

A glass-walled, vibronic decontamination chamber stood nearby. Kyn snorted, dismissing her trapped prey. A swift prowl of the lab proper and a survey of the level below revealed no other dangers. She headed for the decontamination unit, slipped in, and began to strip.

After watching Kyn dispose of Ben Harriman, Anja stepped into the lab and shut the entrance. Her palm pressed against the entry panel, the skin glowing where it met glass. When Ben's cries for help ceased, Anja transmitted the last of her encryption commands and glanced in his direction. He was staring slack-jawed at a topless Kyn struggling out of her trousers inside a decontamination shower. He then noticed Anja, and his pale skin whitened more.

Anja concluded her work on the doors and approached. "You've made a replica of me. Where is she?"

Ben shrank.

"I mean no harm." Anja halted.

"Where's Dirk?" Ben demanded. The glass misted from his breath. "He was going to get help."

"I am sorry," Anja said quietly. "But your friend did not survive."

"You're lying," he said.

Anja studied Ben's face as he absorbed the knowledge.

"Kip's dead too, isn't he?" Ben's lip trembled, and he pushed up his glasses. "My buddies are dead." He curled up within the rejuvenator and pressed fingers to his eyes.

The Femflesh dolls remained facing the doors, unmoved. Anja analyzed Ben's features, her ocular analysis returning physiological signs of his limbic system being overwhelmed. His creased forehead and pulled up eyebrows; the downward turns of his mouth's corners and his quivering chin. He seemed genuinely distressed.

Yet Kyn had warned her of actors and of guilty people who indulged in remorse. Aine the Fifth, the lauded peacemaker, had understood the nuances. If Anja once possessed her predecessor's psychological acuity, she'd lost it in her fall.

Kyn would know better if Ben were acting.

Anja glanced at the decontamination shower. Kyn glared and pointed at the control panel outside her unit.

Anja popped open Ben's hatch and helped the weeping man out.

What are you doing? Kyn demanded. *You were the one who thought he killed Fisher.*

I don't know. Let him try to kill us, then we'll know, Anja signed.

FINE. Kyn pointed at the control panel again.

Anja walked over and activated it for a brisk vibratory cycle. Cleansing vibrations hummed to life and ran sound rings up and down Kyn's body. Particles lifted and flew. Kyn smiled and raised her arms to run her fingers through her flying hair.

Ben joined Anja and wiped his reddened eyes. He stared at Kyn's armpits, and then lower.

Guy's never seen a bush, Kyn remarked to Anja.

"Where is my duplicate?" Anja asked Ben. Her hands also spoke to Kyn.

Why did you undress? The decontamination vibronics can cleanse clothes on the body.

Kyn merely grinned.

"Oh…she's here. She's my stage three Femflesh," Ben wearily said, but pride colored his voice. "These five girls are my stage two."

"Stage three," Anja repeated.

"Stage three is when they can talk. Real conversations showing independent thought. Maybe better than you."

Anja's eyes widened. Kyn was busy holding up her trousers for cleansing, the vibronics too loud for her to follow the conversation. But Kyn's gaze narrowed when she noticed Anja's expression. She hit the *End* button inside the unit and popped the door open.

"Who helped you build my duplicate?" Anja asked as Kyn pulled on her trousers. Kyn then padded over, barefoot, her dirty boots remaining in the shower. She caught Anja's head by the chin. Licking her thumb, she rubbed out the white bloodstain on Anja's forehead.

"Help? I didn't need help, the erotic tech here finally made it easy." Ben wiped his nose on his sleeve, his sorrow momentarily forgotten. Rounding a workstation, he changed the holo display from various surveillance windows of the outside lab to Femflesh data.

"Kip found this building, a bio-geneticist's old hideout. And all her equipment was still here. And the research! When I went through it, I realized we could do it—we could make girls!" He picked up drawings of pony-tailed women in skin-tight latex outfits and showed them to Anja. Kyn pulled on her black tee. "I—I started designing beyond the boring kind of girls—making ones I remembered from a video game. And then Dirk wanted demon girls—"

"These have facial features," Anja said, indicating the drawings.

"Yeah, but Dirk didn't care for simuladildonics, so it wasn't necessary to make them verbally respond and blink and stuff. Mostly to save time and cost. All he wanted was the basic doll body with the basic response. He figured we could unload units faster that way, make fast cash, then shut the operation and reopen with something different. He didn't understand what we could do with this flesh tech. What we could achieve—"

Has he ever gone outside? Kyn asked Anja.

"Nothing like our Femflesh models existed in Darque-world. We could—"

Kyn's hand slammed through the holo projection, cracking

the workstation's surface. Ben jumped.

How to end them? she demanded.

"W-what?" he cried. "I don't know *sign language*."

"She is asking for the fleshmorphs' kill switch," Anja said.

"Kill my *girls?* Are you nuts?"

Kyn's hands moved slowly.

They—are not—girls. Fire ignited in her eyes.

Ben scurried back and looked at Anja. Anja regarded Kyn in turn, concerned.

"W-we have nothing like that," Ben said weakly. "They're only flesh."

Kyn didn't like Ben's smell.

Or she simply didn't like him—the lab he and his buddies took, the fake women he'd made. The glass encased flesh-growing materializer she'd spotted in the lab's lower area reeked of artificial blood and meat despite being empty. Sealed biohazard containers holding flesh-waste sat piled on an elevator platform near the materializer. They were destined for the bio-waste converters beneath the lower level—not genetic by-products, Kyn was certain, but mistakes. Kyn didn't believe that was how Makepeace and Janes were made.

How were you born? she'd asked Aine the Fourth.

As thou were born, Aine lightly answered. *In a cauldron and pulled from starfire.*

Kyn had been born conventionally, the last pup to drop from her mother's womb. Perhaps that was as miraculous as a Perfect's divine cauldron.

"Yet you are able to give the Femflesh commands," Anja pressed.

"The basic fleshmorphs are just dolls to, you know. There's no need for commands."

"I understand that they're simply pleasure aids, but they move beyond basic functions."

"Yeah, but only to—you know."

Why can't you say *it?* Kyn exclaimed. *You're a vulva designer and* robophiliac.

"What—what kind of hand sign is *that?*" Ben ejected.

"Ben Harriman, how do you command these units?" Anja gestured to the five, silent sex dolls.

Ben picked up a white handheld box with red and blue control buttons. "This is how." He activated the unit, and his thumbs danced. The Femflesh dolls slowly turned to face him and the lab, toy pistols still in hand. They leisurely advanced.

"See?" Ben ceased pressing buttons, and the dolls stopped.

Kyn glowered as Anja slowly exhaled.

"Please summon my duplicate," she requested.

"What are you going to do when you see her?" Ben demanded. "As an older model you may not like being replaced."

You can't improve on the gods' perfection, Kyn snapped, *you little ass-molding, jiggle ogling—*

"What? *What?*" Ben yelled. "I'm not putting sign language on my Id!"

Motherfucker—Kyn threw the word from her chin and then shot her hand for Ben's throat.

Anja caught Kyn's wrist. Ben scrambled away.

"Kyn," Anja said softly. Kyn shrugged off her grasp. She stalked across the lab to where large fridge units lined a wall.

"What is the matter?" Anja's voice was low as she followed her.

Little creep, Kyn ejected.

Is he the 'creep' Kip's fiancée referred to? Anja's hands asked.

Kyn's hand swept to encompass the lab. *Do you see another creep here?*

She opened a wall fridge's door. Bright lights lit white shelves within, lined with bio-engineered tissues of different colors, candy pink among them. But beneath the rows of trays, the very bottom shelf held a collection of stacked jars blocked by a cardboard box.

Kyn knelt and hauled the box out as Anja joined her. The labeled jars contained cotton swabs, used tissues, cigarette butts with lipstick on the tips—

Kyn shared a gaze with Anja: genetic samples.

Anja rotated one containing a black hair clipping. The handwritten label read: *girl in park*.

I guess the robophiliac did go out, Kyn said.

What has upset you? Anja asked.

Kyn glanced sideways at Ben who, looking lost and afraid, was comforting himself in the loose-limbed embrace of his dolls. Though he stared warily in Kyn and Anja's direction, he did not appear to be plotting their murder...yet.

No one should create others to be played with, Kyn said.

"But what of purpose?" Anja softly asked. "You and I, the Makepeace and Janes, perform a function."

Duty is different, and I have a mother.

Kyn immediately regretted the remark. But Anja, like most biomechanical beings, had never yearned for conventional birth and family.

Anja smiled. "Ben's playthings are only facsimiles substituting for intimacy. I know now that I am nothing like them."

But he made a synth-flesh copy of you, Kyn angrily said. *That's just like the gods. Everyone* fucking *with you.*

"I do not feel fucked," Anja said evenly.

Kyn grasped Anja's hand.

She would have found Anja's use of profanity adorable, but right then Kyn's heart and mind rode a rollercoaster. She was repeating the same fight she'd had with Aine-5, who, obedient servant that she was designed to be, did not forsake her divine purpose but followed it to her senseless end. It was a fight Kyn never had the chance to say sorry for.

This. Kyn held up Anja's hand. The hieroglyph of the divine holarchy subtly glowed beneath Anja's skin. *At least Artificials are allowed to end duty and have a life.*

"I am making a life," Anja said, confused.

Kyn stood up, bringing Anja with her.

"Why did you leave?" Anja suddenly asked.

I told you.

"When I fell from the celestial realm, I think I landed on my head. I have been nothing but inadequate at understanding you."

It was time to part, and you agreed with me.

"You had mistaken shock at your leaving with acquiescence, which was convenient for you."

Kyn turned away and opened the second fridge door. Seeing more artificial tissue samples, she moved to close it. Anja held the door firmly open and peered at an empty shelf. She then allowed it to close, her silver-eyed gaze on Kyn.

"You had always made the decisions, because in our relationship, my ability to understand it and you was immature. I could only determine what happened after the fact."

Exasperated, Kyn opened a third fridge door. Dark beer bottles met her scrutiny. She then pointed at a thick steel box with a biometric lock, welded to the bottom of the unit: a safe.

"I've already found what I need. Close the door."

Kyn stared, bewildered, but Anja continued.

"We parted during a fight. A very bad one. You let me believe it was because I'd become independent. Assured."

Kyn blew breath. *Yes.*

"Which meant I would no longer listen to you. Need you. You would no longer be able to control me."

Yes.

"You *have never* controlled an Aine. When I was weak, you had been nothing but giving. You can't even look me in the eye when you answer."

Kyn looked at her.

"What have I done?" Anja softly asked.

You keep dying, Kyn snapped.

She turned away, seeing no more fridge doors. Anja's hand slipped beneath Kyn's arm. Her fingers rested beneath Kyn's breast and against the spread of her serratus muscles; a touch like Aine-4's. Kyn trapped the hand close before she could prevent the motion.

I need a break from you, Kyn said painfully.

"Death never stopped your love before," Anja whispered.

Loyal hound, Aine-4 praised.

Kyn turned and took hold of Anja's face.

Their mouths met, Kyn's lips seeking oblivion as Anja's tried to answer her. Kyn's hands spoke even as she desperately kissed her.

I can't stay. I can't.

Anja pulled her mouth away.

"Stop." She stepped back, her breath ragged. "I can't comfort you right now."

Kyn flinched, her insides turned bleak. Anja's gaze searched hers.

"You never gave me this look when you left," she said soft-ly. Her lights winked, a staccato rhythm. "This is more than needing a 'break.' But we don't have time to argue. I must show you something."

Anja opened the second fridge door and reached into the empty shelf. Her hand disappeared, the air glitching. She pulled her hand out from the disrupted holo projection with a sealed test tube in her grasp.

The label read: *Angel*.

Within, shining drops of Perfect blood levitated.

"I saw this in my duplicate's files," Anja said.

Kyn gripped Anja's arm.

The lab doors slid open.

A woman entered, her skin dark and golden beneath her sleeveless gown. An unruly lock of her shining hair waved over one silver-orbed eye. She stepped as one bored or sim-ply dreaming.

Her heavy-lidded gaze met Kyn's.

Recognition lit her silver eyes.

CHAPTER FIVE

"Ann," Ben cried. "I'm so glad you're safe."

He hurried to the woman whose subdermal trace lights at her temple slowly increased illumination, white and bright. Then Ben stopped short, his body shrinking like one scolded. But the woman he called Ann kept her gaze on Kyn even as she reached out and absentmindedly touched Ben's cheek, her gesture gentle. When her hand dropped, her lights faded to glimmering, and her mouth slowly widened.

Anja's double smiled.

Kyn's heart pounded.

She was a real woman. Kyn did not have to touch her to know she was not Femflesh but biomechanical. When Kyn inhaled, she smelled two Anjas in the room.

The clone glanced at the test tube in Anja's hand.

"By their luminescence will ye know them, for their blood shall lift." She spoke in High Celestial, her syllables ringing. Ben covered his ears in bewilderment.

Anja pocketed the test tube.

"No greeting, sister?" The clone reverted to common mortal speech.

"Sister." Anja's tone was pensive. Her twin captured Kyn's gaze again.

"I am Aine the Seventh," she announced.

Kyn swiftly pulled Anja behind her.

Aine-7's smile widened again as if Kyn had performed an adorable antic. The genial warmth drew Kyn, its fondness achingly familiar. It was the smile of Aine the Fourth and Fifth.

"Why were you outside the safety of the lab?" Anja asked from behind Kyn.

"Why?" Aine-7 slowly stepped towards them, bare feet brushing the floor. Her smile gentled, but a hint of teeth gleamed. "I left to help Kip and Dirk. As Ben knows."

Ben, apparently wishing no part in the conversation, hurriedly retreated to an enclosed office overlooking the lab's lower level. His dolls trailed after him.

Aine-7 cocked her head at Anja, amused. "You locked this lab and encrypted its entry code."

"I had assumed you could not resist a cipher," Anja said.

Realization dawned, and Kyn glared at Anja. The stray Anja-scent she'd detected by the generators—

Aine-7's gaze turned mirthful. "An intelligence test? You did not tell Kyn that you suspected I might be roaming."

Anja turned to Kyn. "I did not know until I saw mention of my blood sample in her file," she assured.

Still—Kyn began.

"Why didn't you reveal yourself to us and Fisher?" Anja demanded, returning her attention to her double.

"I'm here now. But as to before...I was uncertain of my reception." Aine-7 met Kyn's gaze. Her expression was inscrutable, but her subcutaneous lights lit like tiny stars.

"Aine the Fifth kept her existence from Kyn, and for good

reason," Aine-7 said.

It was for no good reason.

Anja promptly left her duplicate's presence, dragging a Kyn turned to stone. If Kyn was re-experiencing the hurt Aine-5 had caused her, Anja—despite the fall on her head—could recall it with her. Aine-4's loss had halved Kyn, a hellhound without her shining huntress. Aine-5, marked for assassination and knowing she'd little time left to fulfill her duty, thought it best Kyn not know she existed.

A futile and foolish decision, considering that Aine the Fifth's role as emissary made her known throughout the intragalaxy. Anja wondered if she would have made the same mistake, miscalculating a love's need to speak to her dead.

I missed you, Kyn had lamented to Aine-5 on Nuit 6, a dirge weighing her grieving hands. Not long after their reunion, Aine-5's life abruptly ended too.

Ben fussed in a workstation's drawer, his dolls slowly filing into the office behind him. Beyond the office, the lab's lower level lay with its materializer and piled containers of flesh-waste. He shut the drawer when Anja neared.

"There is a reason clone-tech is safeguarded." She pointed at the stacked biohazard containers below. "The mistakes are costly. The only time you successfully regenerated a genetic sample was with my stolen blood and this—" Her palm's interface summoned copied holo-data. "—The cloning procedure that was somehow given to you."

"I don't know who sent that," Ben said, low.

Kyn grabbed the front of his shirt.

"*I don't*," he cried.

Anja's firm grip on Kyn's wrist made her drop Ben. He quickly backed away, bumping against his office's window. Inside, the dolls stared through the glass.

Their focused gazes, Anja thought, somehow seemed aware.

"My duplicate is hardly like me," she said. Aine-7's own gaze bored into Anja's back right then. "Did you attempt to alter her?"

"See that?" Ben waved at the gleaming genetic sequencer poised next to the materializer's empty glass case and bed. It was a uniquely assembled machine, unlike any model Anja knew. "That amazing piece of flesh-tech? Of course I did. I wanted to fix Ann's eyes and nose, and her mouth, and her skin color, but—"

And her personality? Kyn demanded. Anja touched Kyn's chest, stilling her.

"But?" Anja asked Ben.

"But the genetic coding kept reverting. It was like Ann had to be Ann and resisted improvement."

Kyn's chest vibrated, her vision grown red. Anja's palm pressed.

How great thy heart, Aine the Fourth once said, pressing her palm to the spot. *'Tis my favorite part.*

Kyn stilled.

"Perfects are as the gods make them," Anja said to Ben. "And you are no god. I've learned all I needed to know. This ends now."

Call out, Kyn told Anja.

"I must lift the lockdown blocking communications. I will

try from this station," Anja said.

Ben dashed for his office. The door slid shut and locked as Kyn slammed into it.

"Ben Harriman, what are you doing?" Anja raised her palm and activated the workstation while Ben tapped feverishly on his desk's holo interface. Kyn pried at the sealed door.

The lab's entrance blared, red alert lights flashing. Steel airlock doors screamed and slammed shut over the outer doors. Their rubber seals hissed and inflated.

While alarm bells rang, Kyn stared at Anja.

"I did not do that," Anja said.

"No one's notifying anybody," Ben yelled above the din. "Not until you promise to leave my girls alone."

A quick check in the computer proved what Ben had done: the lab's emergency quarantine had been activated. Anja turned off the alarms and flashing lights and accessed the entrance's security code, only to encounter a familiar cryptographic language.

She glanced at her watchful double.

"You have not thought this through," Anja then said to Ben.

"My girls are all I got. You killed Dirk and Kip," Ben accused.

Kyn and Anja raised brows and shared a look.

"Isn't it more logical to have killers like Kyn leave rather than lock them in with you?" Anja asked.

Kyn huffed and grabbed Anja. She marched her across the lab to the entrance, the dolls and Aine-7's gaze following.

"Kyn, I can break the lock from the workstation we left,"

Anja protested.

"Leave my girls alone, or you'll never get the access code to get out of here," Ben yelled.

Little prick, Kyn said and slapped Anja's palm against the entrance's access panel. Data entered Anja's hand and spun before her ocular interface. Then Kyn whirled, placing herself before Anja.

Aine-7's hips gently swayed as she approached. She slowly blinked at Kyn, a soft smile on her lips.

Kyn leaned back into Anja.

"The cipher is also a puzzle," Anja murmured, her other hand finding Kyn's waist.

"I encrypted the lock for Ben. Perhaps you can't resist the challenge?" Aine-7 halted at a distance that did not threaten Kyn's perimeter. Her warm gaze remained on Kyn even as she spoke to Anja.

Anja moved back. Leather squeaked as she slipped off Kyn's jacket. She evaded Kyn's grasp for her braces and strolled purposefully back to Ben's office. Kyn hurried after, Aine leisurely following. At the workstation they'd left, Anja neatly folded, then draped the jacket on the chair's back.

"Unlock the lab doors," she told Ben.

"Not until you promise to—" Ben yelled.

Kyn slammed her palm against the office's thick glass.

"Give Kyn time and she will break it," Anja said evenly.

"Ben has cause to be fearful, and not of Kyn." Aine-7 slowly rounded the workstation. "Authorities may euthanize his creations."

"He should have thought of that before making you," Anja answered. Kyn's gaze darted between Anja and her twin as her clone passed behind her. Aine-7's hand dropped to idly caress Kyn's jacket.

Anja pointed to the lower level.

"Kyn, please dismantle the flesh-tech and render the machines useless," she requested, "beginning with the sequencer."

"You can't do that." Ben sputtered. "That stuff is mi—"

"It is stolen," Anja said, "and your friends died for this lab."

Anja's harsh words did not surprise Kyn. Unlike her predecessors, Anja was far less considerate in her honesty. But Aine-7's brief smile at Anja's words surprised her.

Aine-7 turned away and held the railing that overlooked the lower level. She leaned on it like one admiring a sunset.

Ben shrank back into his office. His dolls, seemingly no longer interested in those outside, also turned away. Anja focused on her workstation. Kyn stood, hands clenched, searching for air ducts and other escape routes. Anja would protest, but she and her clone needed to leave. Kyn expected a Skycourt security team to swarm them at any second to secure the Anja copy they'd always wanted. How else did Ben get a sample of Anja's blood?

The presence of the airlock doors indicated the lab was Bio-Safety Level 3, a maximum-security quarantine. The air duct system would be a self-contained labyrinth with banks of powerful filters leading only to an air recycling system.

FUCK. Kyn threw both hands from her chin.

Why aren't you taking the equipment apart? Anja signed.

When we first entered, did you lock us in to keep your clone out, or Skycourt? Kyn demanded.

Both, Anja said. Aine-7 moved for the steps leading to

below.

You could have told me, Kyn said.

"You were busy cleansing yourself gratuitously," Anja said aloud and returned her attention to the holo interface.

Aine-7 glanced back as she descended, her fond smile amused. Kyn swallowed—

Aine's silvered eyes sparkled.

Kyn suppressed her desire to bound for her, tail furiously wagging.

Anja waved within Kyn's peripheral vision, and Kyn's head snapped back to her.

You are developing empathy for Seventh, Anja's hands stated.

Well, she's you, Kyn said cautiously.

She is my facsimile, Anja said.

You are the sixth Aine, Kyn said. *Aren't you a copy too?*

She had not meant that the way she'd worded it. Anja's gaze was more weary than angry.

I am as the gods made Perfects—her hands said—*fashioned from a piece of the first Aine. By her own naming and the presence of my blood, we know Seventh is not a Femflesh. But this is more than illegal cloning. You've protected me since she entered, and for good reason.*

Kyn furtively glanced to where Aine-7 waited below.

There can be no Aine the Seventh unless I am dead, Anja said.

When Anja focused on a task, she did so to the detriment of conversation. Her concentration was as much on her invisible, ocular data as well as on what scrolled on the workstation's holo interface. While she worked on Aine-7's cipher, Ben ignored them all and played with his control box, programming his dolls to swing their bodies in an odd dance.

Their breasts swayed. Kyn nearly struck the glass again.

Prying Ben out of his office seemed wasted effort, especially with the seals at quarantine strength. Anja would break the cipher soon enough. Kyn decided to do as she was told.

She was retrieving a toolbox by the fridge units when Aine-7 wandered back up the stairs and crossed the lab floor. Her erect nipples pushed against the thin material of her gown.

Kyn licked her bottom lip and looked away.

"Would you like an ale?" Aine-7 opened the third fridge door.

She did not pick out a dark beer bottle but knelt, pressing a thumb to the biometric lock of the safe. Its thick door whispered open. Within, tall black bottles of Bleeding Scoundrel stood along with packages of medical ampoules and bottles for injections. A tiny vial sitting to the fore caught Kyn's attention.

"Fisher's stash," Aine simply said.

Kyn grabbed the vial and trotted quickly to Anja. She showed her the label.

"Are you suggesting I need that?" Anja said.

NO. No-no-no, Kyn repeated.

"A libido booster." Anja returned her attention to her work. "An archaic formula in liquid form. One for hyposexual females."

It was with other medical stuff—

"Med-kit?" Anja asked.

*Trauma kit. Heart attack, a-n-a-p-h-y-la—a-d-r-e-na—*Kyn gave up spelling and pointed at the vial. *This is what drove the fleshmorphs crazy.*

"No, as Fisher had said, the Femflesh units were meant to lie back and think of England."

This can't make them crazy?

"No, this is not like Rock Hard, which directly engorges the sexual organs. The drug in that vial stimulates the neurotransmitters of the brain controlling response and desire for pleasure. There is no libido to enhance if there is no brain, Kyn, which proves you have one."

The creep gave them to his toys, Kyn said. She suspected the drug's true use but she wanted Anja to say it. Anja plucked the vial from her hand.

"His stage two dolls do not have brains." She rolled the vial between her fingers. "This was meant for the clones he wanted to grow from his genetic samples."

Kyn could not help glancing at Aine-7, who watched them.

"Do you recall how slow I was to become a woman?" Anja suddenly asked.

You were a babe. Reborn upon impact. It was the only way Kyn could explain Anja's fragile and amnesic state when she first saw her in Skycourt's medlab, possessing barely a self or identity.

"My asexual stage was frustrating," Anja murmured. She placed the vial on the desk.

No. Natural, Kyn insisted. Anja had not remained long in a state of innocence. Self-knowledge rapidly woke, trapped in a body and brain that refused to function properly. Kyn had played both nurse and bodyguard during the months Anja spent relearning herself.

She pressed Anja back into her and wrapped her arms. Anja relaxed.

"You were very considerate," she said softly. "Very patient. Then you left."

Kyn hugged tightly.

I must go, Aine-5 had told her. Three nights later, she was forever gone.

Eight years later, Aine the Sixth fell from the heavens.

Over a year after her fall, Anja, who took a variation of her Aine name, told Kyn: *I must go to the stars.*

She did not first say, *let us leave.* She did not say *it is time for something new.*

She had said: I must go.

Within Anja, a secret destiny waited, programmed by celestial hands. Of that, Kyn was certain.

She shut her eyes and breathed Anja in.

Anja gently extricated from Kyn's arms.

"You have a task, Kyn." She refocused on her work. "And please keep her busy."

And please keep her busy.

Anja had murmured the last directive, drawing a raised brow from Aine-7, who lingered by the fridge units. Kyn's heartbeat sped and resounded in her ears.

She jumped the railing for below and landed with a slap of bare feet on the polished floor. Grabbing the genetic sequencer, she heaved. Floor bolts popped when the machine toppled.

Her muscles swelled and her crackling spine elongated. Connection cables whipped as she ripped them from the floor. Seizing the sequencer's head, she wrenched it off and then raked through the insides, ignoring the electrical shocks. She could tear at the machine all day, but irreparable destruction of the machine's primary components required a focused approach.

When Kyn diminished in size, claws and fangs

disappearing, Aine-7 stood before her, two perspiring bottles of Bleeding Scoundrel in hand. Her silver-eyed gaze gleamed, traveling slowly up Kyn's body to her face.

She produced a bottle opener and popped the caps off.

Kyn accepted the ale Aine offered.

We drink to Fisher, Kyn said.

"Very well." They both drank. After one swallow, Kyn upended her bottle. Beer poured on the lab floor; Fisher's portion.

"Did you like him?" Aine asked.

Anja liked him, Kyn said.

Aine smiled and raised her bottle to her lips again.

Anja could barely tolerate intoxication; Aine-5 imbibed moderately and only at public functions. Aine the Fourth drank like the best of warriors.

Aine-7 swallowed her ale as if she enjoyed such libations every day.

"Do you still keep nests of women?" she asked.

Setting her bottle aside, Kyn formed a knife hand. She thrust it swiftly within the sequencer's head, slicing cables, and then yanked a small steel box from the torn innards. Sparks flew.

Yes, she curtly said.

"Ben keeps a comfort circle too."

Kyn glanced at the upper level and marked Anja at her workstation, her back facing the railing. Next to her lay the steps, then Ben's office. At the side window, Ben sat and gaped down at Kyn and Aine. His dolls continued their odd dance.

Kyn hefted the sequencer's head and hurled it.

A smash sounded as it bounced off the window. Cracks surrounded the crushed glass at the impact's center, but with no hole evident. Kyn's gaze narrowed: armored glass, fully layered and graded for Other-being attacks. Ben sat stiffly within as a shield door slowly descended over the damaged window, obscuring him and his dolls from view. Kyn turned back to her work.

No, Kyn said, *it's not the same.*

While Kyn pried at the sealed box with her nails, Aine sat down on the prone body of the sequencer. She hooked Kyn's belt loop with a finger and coaxed her to sit beside her.

"His toys cause no harm."

There's nothing wrong with real women, Kyn snapped. *And biomechanical beings*, she added hastily.

"I understand, Kyn, but enslavement is an old story." Aine-7 smiled, smelling warm and musky. Anja rarely wore clothing that showed cleavage, and when Aine leaned over to rest her elbows on her knees, her skin and softness revealed themselves.

"I should be grateful for that ageless desire to possess and control. If the gods had not wished for servants, I would not be here."

Aine-5 had once said the same thing. Kyn bowed her head and focused on her box.

Aine-7 brushed hair away from Kyn's eyes, startling her.

"Are all Aines in your heart?" she asked softly. Her warmth radiated. "Art thou our loyal hound?"

Kyn's heart jerked. Longing sharpened.

"Yet you chose Aine-6 to forsake...I've pondered why."

Aine's breath touched Kyn's cheek.

"I'm new," she whispered, twining fingers with Kyn's own, "and I am beholden to no destiny that can take me away from you."

She raised their clasped hands, her thumb caressing.

Beneath the skin of Aine's hand, no sacred hieroglyph glowed.

When Kyn smashed Ben's window, it gave Anja an excuse to openly gauge what was happening below.

Kyn was sitting near her clone with upraised hands clasped, apparently having forgotten she was supposed to seduce her. Anja drew a patient breath and returned to her interface.

She had solved the doors' cipher. But more needed to be done to take care of the lab and Aine-7.

Three of Ben's dolls stood mannequin-like at the window, their glassy-eyed attention seemingly focused on her. From their position, they had full view of the surrounding lab. She decided to wait them out.

With the holo screen scrolling as if she were still decoding, Anja perused the data uploaded to her ocular interface. She'd already reviewed the lab's medical inventory and picked what she needed. She then linked to the lab's rejuvenators and overrode their safety charging protocols. Finally, she scanned the lab logs of Ben's cloning failures, seeking more clues about her own clone. Her gaze darkened at one odd entry: brain surgery.

She downloaded the information and introduced a virus. Nuit authorities and Skycourt would not appreciate the destruction, but she in turn did not appreciate the careless creation of Aine-7. If Skycourt was the true culprit behind Femflesh receiving her bio-dats and blood sample, why use amateur synth-flesh technicians to build a copy of herself? The entire scenario was sloppy.

The desk drawer Ben had fiddled with sat askew. She

rattled it open. Atop a paper log book, a pharmaceutical blue bottle of archaic medicine tablets rolled, its label reading: *cyproterone acetate.*

Her internal medical data cache provided a match. *Cyproterone acetate: a synthetic steroidal antiandrogen used to suppress androgenic activity in the body. A treatment for sex drive reduction in sex offenders.*

She flipped through the logbook, grim.

Ben sat hunched with his back to the window. Two dolls loosely embraced before him, their faces close. He was co-ordinating the meeting of their lips. At Anja's approach, the dolls at the window slowly turned their heads to regard her. Anja rapped on the glass.

"Go away," Ben said.

"Did Kip and Fisher know about your cloning attempts?" Anja asked.

"No."

"Tell me how you made Aine-7."

Ben watched his embracing dolls and ignored her.

"I can open your office, Ben Harriman," Anja said. "But I've allowed you to stay where you can't anger Kyn and let her tear out your organs and eat them."

Ben swiveled around, his face white. "W-w—okay, what?"

"I exaggerate. She wouldn't eat your organs." Anja pulled her test tube from her trousers' pocket and held it up. The shining blood drops levitated. "Tell me about this."

"That arrived in a package. An unmarked one. And it was addressed to me." Ben stared at the floating drops. "I knew that blood came from one of you special artificial people. I followed the instructions that got sent...I entered your bio-dats into the materializer, left a drop of that on the bed...the next morning, Ann was there. Fully grown."

It was a miraculous occurrence by conventional cloning standards, but not unexpected from a Perfect's blood.

"What did Kip think when he found out she was not a flesh unit but a clone?"

"He blew his stack," Ben ejected. "He kept going on about artificial sentients rights and how we're all sex slavers now. He was going to shut us down."

Anja watched his face, analyzing the physical clues. She pocketed the test tube. "And Fisher?"

"Dirk always tries to keep the peace. He wanted Kip to sleep on it and for me to focus on making basic fleshmorphs…but I bet Dirk was planning to drop Ann off somewhere and give her money to disappear." Ben tone turned bitter. "That's not right. I *made* her."

"You wanted her to stay," Anja said.

"Of course, I did. I—"

"Made her. Before I corrupted your database, I copied your logs regarding Aine-7."

Ben's eyes darted. "I'm not going to—"

"*You* will listen. Darquekind's biomechanical beings first waken in an asexual state. The Makepeace are designed so, and sometimes that is true of Perfects. I was thus for eight months after my fall until I experienced sexual awakening.

"You injected my genetic material with libido boosters, Ben, yet Aine-7 did not awaken the sexual plaything you wanted.

"Failing to influence her libido, you altered her behavior by surgically stimulating her brain's limbic regions. You *induced* hyper-sexuality in Aine-7."

The dolls closed in, crowding her view. Their slow hands clumsily pawed for her. Anja moved to a clear spot at the window and brought up the bottle of anaphrodisiacs. She pressed it where Ben could see, and a crack popped on its surface against the glass. "She frightened you, didn't she? A sexualized woman was not the empty-headed sex puppet you'd envisioned. This, Ben, is for chemical castration, and according to your logs, she has missed today's dose. A hormonal rush is imminent."

—*BAM*—

Anja turned for the lab's entrance, the impact outside the sealed doors dully echoing. When she glanced at Ben, he seemed as baffled as she felt—

—*BOOM*—

And frightened.

CHAPTER SIX

"No matter the kind of Aine created, you love each of us, don't you, Kyn?"

Aine's familiar, intimate voice…it was warmer than Anja's and more knowing. Aine-7's gaze burned. It was a hearth Kyn dared not enter. She pulled her hand away and ripped the box open.

Kyn fumbled to snap and break the contents. Aine picked up her ale and poured it on the box's circuitry. They popped and sizzled, swiftly blackening.

"I've a story." Aine said as Kyn dropped the burning box aside. "One that gives me hope. Would you like to hear it?"

Her gaze trapped Kyn again. Of course she knew Kyn liked stories.

"Once," Aine began, "a hellhound birthed a litter, children of hellfire, and dark gods gathered to pick their hunters. But roughhousing among the strongest offspring was a runt, a weak little pup. A death goddess picked that female up by the throat." Aine held her beer bottle aloft, gripping its neck. "And squeezed for the cull and her sacrifice. The pup's fiery bite on her tightening hand caused that dark one to laugh. She forgave the little one, but not before crushing her larynx, gifting aphonia upon her forever."

Aine touched Kyn's throat.

"*Kólasi Kynigós.*" The syllables of Kyn's true name rang in the air. "Hell huntress."

Kyn's blood thundered.

"I've thought about this, Kyn. Of why the gods flung the sixth Aine down like Hephaestos, rejected. She can't remember, but you suspect.

"Fourth defied the gods, even as they caused her end. Fifth abided and followed duty until her assassination. But Sixth—"

Kyn abruptly rose, only for Aine's grip to jerk her down again.

"Shh," Aine soothed, and touched Kyn's lips. "I won't tell her. But I have to know."

Shut up, Kyn said.

—BAM—

Something struck the lab doors—Kyn's gaze swiveled to the level above. Anja was not at the workstation.

—BOOM—

What—

A sharp pull on her chin brought her gaze to Aine's again. "I'll say it, then. Did you leave lest she proved the gods' judgment, that she is less than perfect?"

—BANG-BANG-BANG—

Kyn twisted away. That sound was no battering ram—

Anja stood at the railing, unperturbed by the pounding outside. She studied Kyn and her clone, her calm regard sharp.

What's happening? Kyn said up to her.

Aine took hold of Kyn's face again. Her warm breath touched Kyn's lips.

Kiss her, Anja's hands said.

What? No, Kyn wanted to shout.

—*BAM-BAM*—

—*THUMP*—

"All Aines have a purpose, Kyn." Aine forced Kyn's gaze to lock with hers. "Sixth is—"

Shut UP, Kyn said.

"She is the *failure*. Yet, mistake that she is, she still has purpose. And when that purpose is done—what then? Did the gods tell you to *cull* her?"

NO, Kyn said, even as Aine held her wrists fast. Kyn sought Anja—

Aine the Fourth stood at the railing, her winged helm and armor shining.

Thou preoccupy her, she said, her lips unmoving.

—*BUMP-BUMP-BUMP*—

"It's all right, Kyn," Aine-7 fiercely whispered. "It'll be okay."

She repeated the promise between kisses, engaging Kyn's mouth until no more words issued. Kyn succumbed to softness and heat that sucked breath away. She gasped against a mouth that consumed. Aine's hands ran beneath Kyn's shirt, nails raking. Soon, Kyn had no shirt, and Aine's fingers were undoing Kyn's belt buckle, unzipping her, and then tugging her trousers down to dig into Kyn's bared ass.

Kyn did not notice when the pounding on the doors silenced.

—THUMP—

Anja would have winced but she'd no time for Kyn's ire. She turned away before Kyn could yell at her and summoned the surveillance system.

The cams outside the lab showed nothing but blackness. As far as she could tell, the cams were dead. Security surveillance beyond their location—into the basement corridors, stairwells, and floors above—revealed no invading presences.

—BUMP-BUMP-BUMP—

"Wh-what's going on? What's happening?" Ben cried. His dolls moved aimlessly and stumbled. One fell over the desk.

Anja checked the lockdown's status; nothing had broken it. Her scrutiny of the lab doors with zoomed vision assessed that no breach was yet evident. She disabled the lockdown and called Nuit Four's security.

When the call failed, she rechecked the lockdown's status—she'd freed the building.

My Id's communicator hasn't worked even before all hell broke loose, Fisher had said.

The signal cloak: it had nothing to do with the lockdown.

Flesh smacked against metal, and Anja looked below. Aine-7 was naked.

Aine had cleared a lab table. Kyn lay beneath her on the metal tabletop while their mouths battled. Their legs and arms tangled for dominance. Aine thwarted Kyn's attempt to flip her over, and her flexed thigh dragged up Kyn's crotch, stroking hard. Kyn reared.

Anja turned away. Inside Ben's office, the dolls at the window collided into each other. Their mouths met, teeth tearing synthetic flesh. Anja ran across the lab for the refrigerated safe.

Kyn's bare ass struck metal with Aine holding her down.

Aine-7 was stronger than Anja—as strong as Aine-5. Kyn yielded to her frenzied need, and Aine rode Kyn's thigh.

If Kyn were allowed to speak, she would encourage: *baby, come, come—*

Aine flipped her. She rubbed herself on Kyn's ass. Her fingers found their way inside Kyn and her teeth sank into her shoulder. Kyn held on to the table's sides with her nipples burnishing steel. Aine was a jackhammer. Then Kyn found herself flipped into the air and body-slammed, her back denting metal.

"Take it—take it—take it—" Aine fiercely urged.

Her wildly moving hand found sweetness. Her brow's lights blinded. Kyn came hard enough for her nails to draw blood from Aine's shoulders. The shining blood drops rose in the air as Kyn's vision whitened and then returned.

Aine mounted her face. Their six and nine coupling was a war of frantically working mouths. Kyn came again, and Aine took more. Aine never rested. Each climax seemed a test on how much pleasure she could summon, how much she could devour. Her appetite was greater than Kyn could—

She threw off Aine's legs around her head only for them to return. Twisting her hips, she could not dislodge her. Kyn scrambled with Aine's mouth never letting go—

FUCK, Kyn ground out. *Get* off *me—*

She put her curled thumb and forefinger inside her mouth and blew two shrill blasts.

Kyn's safe-sound—her signal to stop sex play—pierced the lab's air. Anja abandoned the transformer she was tampering with and sped for the railing. Vaulting, she saw Kyn heave and flip Aine-7 over. The back of Aine's head banged against the metal table. Kyn slid atop and held Aine down by the wrists. She raked her crotch along Aine's abdomen.

Anja landed with her soles thunder clapping. She reached into her trousers' pocket for the hypo-injector she'd prepared.

The two grappled on the lab table, their breaths fast and heavy between open-mouthed kisses. Aine bucked, and Kyn pressed down harder, her heavy-lidded gaze flashing red fire. Laughing, Aine braced her feet and thrust her body up. Kyn fell back, and Aine-7 grabbed her face.

Anja removed her hand from her pocket. She stepped quickly for the elevator platform and its stacks of bio-waste containers. When she hit the button for descent, a palm loudly slapped the lab table's surface two times—

Anja stiffened. Another signal from Kyn to stop sex play.

On the table, Aine-7 had regained top position, her groin smothering Kyn's face and her arms trapping Kyn's legs. Aine's lowered head was a blur. Kyn gripped the table's sides with veined arms. Metal squealed and dented beneath her shaking hands.

Anja's own hand trembled as she reached into her pocket again.

Not in front of Kyn.

The platform sank like the sickening drop in her stomach. Bile rose. She reached the maintenance level with her equilibrium parameters readjusting her physiological reactions. The violent coupling continued noisily above. Bio-waste processing machinery hummed serenely around her, and she heard no more safe-signals from Kyn.

A matter recycler stood, tall, fat, and faintly roaring. Straightening, she approached stiffly and keyed its maw open. As the jaws parted, the roar grew. A cyclone of light whirled within, an oven large enough for bodies. She heaved a flesh-waste container into it.

With a scream, the recycler decimated the container into flying particles.

Anja keyed the jaws closed. If Kyn's sacrifice was to mean anything, she needed to work quickly. The fingers of her right hand split and extended tools. She rapidly unfastened and removed the panel of the recycler's control unit.

Aine-7 seemed bent on wringing every orgasm possible from Kyn's body.

She took mercy before Kyn could black out from the sheer intensity. The power in the limbs conquering her, the sun-like body heat—it was as if Aine the Fourth was straddling Kyn, but one gone mad with maenadic lust. Ravenous.

And in the confusion of coming and tasting and scent, coming and gasping and flesh, Aine was also somehow Anja, but with lights like piercing diamonds.

Aine-7 bit Kyn's throat.

The noise of flesh on flesh ceased, and heat dissipated from skin. Kyn lay with her senses open to the entire lab—its cool and still sterility—and thought the place entirely unaffected by the savage sybaritism it had witnessed.

Aine ran a hand from Kyn's sensitive crotch up to her throat, and then slipped off the table, her warmth gone. Kyn watched her, uncertain, as she wandered away towards her tossed dress.

Kyn sat up and winced.

She was pulling her tee over her body and covering the long, bleeding scratches made by Aine's nails, when Anja slowly descended the steps, Kyn's leather jacket in hand. Her subdued gaze avoided Kyn's eyes.

She laid the jacket on the lab table where carnality had repeatedly dented the metal only moments before. Then she picked up Kyn's trousers and handed them to her. After gingerly pulling them on, Kyn tried to catch her gaze.

"If you are harmed, I am sorry," Anja whispered. Kyn grasped her hand.

I wasn't violated, she assured. *I'm not hurt.*

Anja's gaze drifted to the bite on Kyn's throat, and then looked away. Kyn tried again.

It was rough, but you know I like that.

It had been more than rough. She felt hit by a truck. Anja swallowed and nodded.

Aine-7 meandered near. The zipper of Kyn's leather jacket scraped metal. Aine slowly pulled a sleeve of Kyn's jacket on like a supple, second skin. Once she fully donned the jacket, she hugged the leather to herself and stepped away.

Who was outside? Kyn asked Anja.

"I don't know. The lockdown was not breached, and the surveillance cams outside and throughout the building revealed nothing."

Did you open the doors and look?

Anja raised a brow. "You would have told me not to."

Though the question of what had attacked the lab doors

nagged, Kyn couldn't help smiling. A glance marked Aine yards away and with her back to them, her body slowly swaying as if lost in private thoughts.

What did I sacrifice my body for? Kyn asked teasingly.

"I've timed the lab's transformer to overload and deactivated the fire suppression system. When it explodes, the resulting fire should damage most of the lab. The lockdown is also disengaged. Here is our route out." Anja projected a holo-map from her palm. In the bio-waste converter room below, a maintenance tunnel led away from the building and into the Pong's own tunnels. "We'll leave as soon as I speak with my clone—alone," she emphasized.

Kyn frowned. What Anja shared didn't sound like actions needing Aine-7's ignorance.

"Not all my questions here have been answered," Anja continued before Kyn could ask her more. "And perhaps never will."

Her weighted comment, aimed directly at Kyn, seemed to speak of more than the mystery of how Aine-7 came to be.

Kyn sighed, and Anja looked at her expectantly.

When Anja opened her mouth, Kyn shushed her.

I left you because of a vision, she said.

"A visitation." Anja's gaze sharpened. "What did they tell you?"

When Kyn said nothing, Anja took a deep breath. "You won't tell me."

I'm trying to figure it out.

"Let me help." Anja's searching gaze then dawned with perception. "By keeping me in ignorance, I am helping," she clarified. "As usual, you are wrong."

Kyn's eyes widened, exasperated. *Listen to me. You are Aine.*

"I am Anja."

You—Kyn tried to find words. Why was she always the one who had to explain stuff to Anja?

You are the sacrifice, Kyn said, pleading with Anja to understand. *You're the death giving Heimdallr's horn reason to sound and the celestial heavens to darken. You become the chalice heroes follow. You're life-giver.*

All Perfects have a greater purpose. And for that purpose, you die.

"You think that like Aine-5 I will sacrifice myself soon, and your heart cannot take that."

The accusatory tone surprised Kyn.

Baby, she said.

"Not only am I not Fourth, I am not Fifth. You never allowed me to tell you that...or prove it."

Kyn fastened her belt buckle as she climbed the steps for the upper level, dejected.

Anja had brushed lips with her as if to soften the sting of her words. Then she'd turned for Aine-7, who'd found a workstation to fiddle with.

Aine-7 was the tousled picture of an Anja having survived a sexual hurricane. Her skin glowed, and Kyn could smell her arousal still. Aine idly caressed the lapel of Kyn's jacket while her right hand engaged the interface. Kyn decided to chance leaving the two alone since that was Anja's wish and left to investigate the lab's entrance.

"Just hold still," Ben said in his office.

Ugh. Kyn deliberately ignored his window and headed for the lab doors. A wall panel lay aside nearby, revealing a humming transformer. Large enough to cause a small explosion, it would at the very least, start a fire that would gradually destroy most of the lab—if Nuit Four's emergency teams did not respond in time.

Kyn's brow knit. Anja was very thorough. One transformer was not enough for her intentions. She had to have been up to more during all that time Aine-7 was ravishing her. Kyn then turned her attention to the entrance.

The sealed doors held no damage, not even burn marks from a cutter. She recalled the noise from earlier and tried to imagine what weapon could make such erratic sounds... organic sounds.

She laid her hand on the entrance's access panel.

Aine-7 smiled and raised her brows at Anja's approach.

"You deleted everything," she said, deactivating her holo interface. "Thoroughly. As if the fleshmorphs had never been." Her grin and gaze turned inquisitive. "I'm erased."

Anja took a deep breath and looked aside. She flinched when Aine-7 touched her chest.

"You're upset Kyn and I had sex." Aine's tone was soft. "Yet you wanted it to happen."

"I failed to take into account your rapaciousness." Anja turned her attention to the upper level.

"Kyn, retrieve Ben. We will leave soon," she called and walked to the elevator platform.

"Let us speak." Anja pressed the down button. "In private."

At Anja's call, Kyn removed her hand from the access

panel. To her annoyance, Anja hadn't bothered to unlock it. She trotted back to Ben's office, determined not to travel with five mannequins that probably couldn't negotiate corners. Like it or not, the robophiliac would have to leave his toys behind.

"No, no-no-no," Ben ejected within. Three of his dolls leaned against the window, their lips and cheeks oozing white fluid from bites in their artificial flesh.

Kyn slowed. She stopped near one with her torn dress hanging around her waist. The angry, long wheals on her body wept white blood. Kyn lifted her tee and looked at the scratches on her own torso. She and the doll matched.

"Oh come on, lighter! Lighter skin tone!"

Ben sat between two dolls in office chairs, their limbs splayed while he touched one up on the face with a putty knife. He looked up, his white face shaken.

Get out of there, Kyn said.

"No way, you cannibal," he accused.

What—the fuck? Kyn said.

The elevator platform rose, fitting into the ceiling. With a dull clang, it sealed Anja and her clone into the bio-waste converter room. She turned for her twin.

Aine-7's gaze wandered around the red-lit space and rested on the fat body of the gently roaring recycler. The walls softly pulsed, a womb with dead remains.

Aine toed a biohazard canister aside. "What have you been up to?"

"Preparation for the lab's destruction," Anja replied.

"I could have helped."

"I felt you had libidinal needs...requiring attention. Especially after reading your file."

Kyn's leather jacket squeaked. Aine-7 stepped near and ran a finger down the French front of Anja's dress shirt.

"I see. Have you developed a taste for being a cuckquean?" she softly asked. She straightened a button.

Anja swallowed. Aine-7 smelled of Kyn and sex; leather and her own arousal.

Aine cocked her head playfully. "I would have come looking for you. I didn't intend to remain here, their cheap sex object."

"You are more than that." Anja removed Aine-7's hand that caressed her abdomen.

"I am." Aine smiled.

"I think you possess a unique ability beyond that of an Aine."

"Oh? And what's that?"

"Telepsychic influence." Anja watched her carefully. "I've seen how you affect Ben's dolls."

Aine's smile faded.

"It's only the Femflesh that feel your intentions...isn't it?"

Their gazes locked, and Anja steeled herself for a touch on her mind she might not be able to resist.

Aine-7 laughed. Stepping back, she suddenly kicked a container aside, and the flesh-waste sloshed noisily.

"I was formed in the same cauldron as they, perhaps that's how I gained the ability. I could probably make the stinking dregs surrounding us sing." Aine's grin grew bitter. "It would not be a pretty song."

"The Fleshmorphs' escape, and then the deaths...was it you?" Anja asked.

"You've seen Ben's logs, what do you think?" Aine-7

turned away.

"I think he did terrible things to you."

"An understatement." Aine's hushed tone was harsh. "Without medication, my condition is—unmanageable. What happened to Kip—and the man in the salon—and Dirk. They became victims of my instability."

Anja took a breath. "Yet Ben's pills can't have worked."

Aine-7 turned back slowly. "What do you mean?"

For a moment, Anja thought she nearly saw a smile touch Aine's lips.

"You would have built tolerance." Anja's right hand slipped into her trousers' pocket. "And swiftly. We are Perfects and designed to grow more and more so, in strength and resistance, until only gods may strike us down."

Aine-7's eyes lidded. "Like Aine the Fourth."

"Like Aine the Fourth," Anja softly agreed.

Aine-7 stepped near. "What are you trying to say?"

Anja gripped the injector. "You are hyper-sexual. But housed in the same cerebral region for sexual desire is our ability for violence. When Ben invaded your brain, he didn't simply make you wanton. He activated hyper-aggression in you."

White lights intensified upon Aine's brow, brilliant, perfect, and cold. They were sharp like diamond tips.

"Is it a divine joke that I, meant for starfire, should be damaged like some boy's cheap, plastic toy?" Aine demanded, her tone quiet with fury.

"You are Aine-7, and you did not choose to simply walk out of this place. You blacked out communications before Fisher left the lab." Anja breathed, calming her rapidly beating heart.

"Thou took innocent life," she pronounced.

"I awoke in *innocence*."

Anja's back slammed against the wall, the shout a gunshot in her ear. Aine's arm pressed into her throat.

"And they—*they* were not innocent to *me*. Sixth," Aine-7 whispered, "would ye be judge?" Her brows arched, both plea and enticement in her gaze. "How your voice quavered, sister, in making the annunciation."

Anja pressed back with her left arm, the limb trembling with the effort. Her hand's grip measured the compression force of the arm choking her. Ocular analysis assessed that Aine-7's strength was greater than her own.

"Kyn should not decide," Anja said.

Aine-7's mouth twisted, wry. "Agreed. Kyn is not an exterminator."

Anja swung her right fist up for Aine-7's neck.

Aine twisted and grabbed the wrist, forcing Anja to drop the hypo-injector. Aine-7 caught it.

"Sixth," she chided, "and after your talk of ineffective drugs."

She slammed the injector into Anja's chest.

CHAPTER SEVEN

Ben's putty knife clattered against the medical tray.

"And why do your eyes even *do* that?" he complained to Kyn. "Are those some kind of—holo-contacts, to make your eyes look like hell or something?"

Kyn stared at Ben, horrified.

Get the fuck out of—

"I'm not coming out to be your dinner," Ben hollered.

You scrawny little rubber teat *sucker*, Kyn violently said, her motions thumping the glass.

"I don't know what you just signed, but you're this lewd... nasty animal, you know that?" Ben exclaimed, disgusted.

Doll fucker, Kyn ejected.

"Look," Ben cried. "Maybe I don't want to leave with you guys, okay? I just—not with you."

Why, Kyn demanded.

"Not with all of you," he emphasized. He hunched and retrieved his knife. He returned to patching his doll's torn flesh.

Kyn turned away, recalling a trolley she'd seen on her first survey of the lab. A tray of make-up for the dolls lay piled on it, a red lipstick among them. She found the trolley and snatched up the tube. Returning to Ben's office, she uncapped the lipstick.

Kyn rapped on the glass, regaining Ben's attention. Then she wrote across the glass: *Did you kill Kip and Fisher?*

"Wha—why would I do *that?* They're my friends," Ben cried.

Tears started in his eyes, and as if surprised by his own reaction, he stuck fingers beneath his glasses. Ben sobbed, and Kyn did not have to smell his tears to know the truth.

She smacked the glass to make him look at her.

You know who did, she wrote.

"This is *stupid*—"

TELL ME, Kyn said.

Ben stuck fists into his eyes. "There's only me and Ann now, what do you think?" he said tearfully.

Kyn's lipstick snapped against the glass.

A red smear followed her falling hand. She'd suspected.

"Something went wrong." Ben hung his head. "I—I don't think she can help herself. When she's—when she's on the castration drugs, she's actually okay. But today, with the Femflesh escape and the...she missed her dose.

"You like them both, right?" he then said fearfully. "I mean...you're going to end up with one of them, anyway."

Kyn turned and leapt the railing. She ran for the elevator platform.

Anja's pain parameters cut off the nociceptive signals from

her chest and initiated healing protocols. Aine-7's blow had brought down the hypo-injector hard enough to crack her sternum.

"Was the dosage enough to incapacitate me or kill me?" Aine-7 asked lightly. She pulled the injector off and tossed it. "Let's find out."

"We will." Anja's hand slipped into her pocket.

She swung up and stabbed Aine in the neck.

"This is the real injector," she said.

Anja suddenly flew, the breath snatched from her, and the room sped by. She struck the far wall hard enough to rattle her brain. When she hit the floor, scattering bio-waste containers, her ocular mapping was the only thing steady before her shaky vision.

Aine-7 stepped woozily and shook her head. "Quite a— hit, Sixth. Let—let me guess. Was the drug something quaint and mundane? Like you?" She advanced, blinking rapidly. "Morphine?"

"Nitroglycerin." Anja regained her feet and lunged. She grabbed Aine's hand. "This is morphine."

She stabbed the inside of Aine's wrist.

Aine-7's fist crunched into Anja's face, making an audible crack.

When Anja blinked again, she saw only floor and Aine-7's feet, her face radiating pain. Blood ran down the back of her throat and from her broken nose, the drops detaching and levitating into the air.

"Bad...Sixth." Aine-7 grabbed the Y of her braces and dragged her across the floor. Anja grabbed desperately for the arm.

"You've never been hit," Aine exclaimed softly. "A shock, isn't it?" She stopped and activated a panel.

The matter recycler's jaws slid open and its roar deafened. The cyclone of light within illuminated. Aine pulled Anja up by the throat. Perspiration wet Aine-7's brow, and her pupils' dilation drowned the silver irises. She wrenched Anja's right forearm aside while Anja struggled.

"A simple, artificial limb for a simple cripple." Aine-7's grip was unshakeable. "Yet the sacred sign still manifested under your grafted flesh—" She shoved Anja's right hand into the recycler's mouth. "And did not appear on *mine*," she roared.

The recycler screamed as Anja's hand dissolved into particles.

Zzt—

Kyn twisted the stripped wires together. Anja—or Aine-7—had locked the elevator platform from descending. The fact that either of them bothered meant the delay was essential. Kyn's heart hammered.

—WHOMP—

Her head snapped up. That was not an explosion outside the lab doors, but an impact.

—WHUMP—WHAM-WHAM—

The doors would have to hold. She pressed the down button.

Ben screamed.

FUCK, Kyn ejected.

"Help me, *help*," he yelled.

You little fucker—

Kyn jumped off the descending platform and ran for the upper level.

✦

Anja's nervous system shut down communication with her right wrist, the area numbing as her robotic limb self-sealed fluidic and circuitry damage. She trembled in Aine's grip.

Aine-7 watched, fascinated by Anja's reactions.

Her eyes widened as Anja hooked her leg.

A shove to the side of Aine-7's head was sufficient to unbalance her and tip her into the maw. Momentum and weight would force her to fall. The flying ends of Aine-7's hair dissolved into particles.

Horror seized Anja's soul. With a heave, she pulled Aine out.

She held Aine-7's arm and breathed while Aine stared at her.

"Now look who didn't think this through," Aine-7 scolded. She shoved Anja's right arm into the cyclone.

Anja's body seized as her ocular interface flashed red. A body map tracked the rapid disintegration of her forearm. Nociceptors swiftly shut down at her elbow, but not before the feedback sent a tsunami of agony crashing through her brain and body. Aine-7 held her as she collapsed at the foot of the recycler.

"Murder's not easy, Sixth." Through the roar of blood in Anja's ears, Aine-7's soft tones drifted, distant.

—*whomp*—

That—sound? *Kyn?*

"But after the first kill...." Aine-7 smoothed hair away from Anja's face.

—*whump*—*wham-wham*—

"You get used to it," Aine whispered.

The elevator's hydraulics hissed. The platform was

descending. Anja unclenched her teeth.

"Ky—"

Aine smothered Anja's mouth with her hand.

Somewhere above, Ben screamed.

"Guess what?" Aine-7 smiled. "I saved Ben for last."

Anja reached shakily into her pocket.

She stuck another injector into Aine-7's neck.

Kyn swept up a steel chair as she leapt for Ben's office. Her muscles expanded, veins bulging.

—*BAM—BAM-BAM-BAM*—

The lab doors still held. When she reached the window—

"Nooo—NO," Ben cried.

The dolls held him aloft, each clenching a limb and the fifth doll, Ben's head. They pulled, and he wailed.

Kyn swung repeatedly at the glass with rapid-fire blows. Each smashing impact created shattered patterns that spread wider and wider. When the chair exploded into pieces in her hands, Kyn hauled up the workstation desk and threw it.

Glass flew as the desk penetrated the final, weakened layer. Kyn pulled it out and jumped through. She swiped at the two dolls holding Ben's legs and sent their decapitated heads smashing against the wall. Ben shrieked at the sight of her, and the shrill sound made her hackles rise.

With a silent roar, she punched through the chest of the doll gripping Ben's head. Why it didn't simply break Ben's neck, she didn't know. The sole focus of their clumsy limbs seemed to be on tearing Ben—

"*Ahhh*," Ben yelled as one doll wrenched his arm, dislocating his shoulder with a pop. Kyn raked her claws across and severed the doll from her arms. She shoved the remaining dolls aside.

BUMP—BUMP—

"G-get away, don't touch m—*yaaah*—" Kyn snapped Ben's shoulder back into place.

When she dropped him outside the window, he scampered for the lab's entrance.

—BAM—WHUMP—

Little shit—Kyn flung away the dolls groping for her and leapt out after him. A high-pitched whine hit her ears and she looked at the far wall with its removed panel.

Anja's voltage overload, she thought.

"Help, police, there's a monster in here with me," Ben yelled to the entrance.

Kyn brought Ben down and covered him with her body just as the transformer blew, the deafening explosion sending tremors through the floor and blinding fire shooting. Rapid bursts of roaring combustion followed as transformer connections erupted in succession. Sparks spewed and landed on Kyn.

When the noise died down, she let Ben go, and he scrambled away. Smoke and flames rose.

The lab's entrance whooped once, then twice. Ben stumbled for it. A hiss sounded as the airlock doors depressurized and slid open.

Kyn blinked.

Ben screamed again.

CHAPTER EIGHT

Sounds of—window—smashing—Kyn was taking forever to smash a window. Anja tottered away from the recycler. Behind her, Aine-7 swayed where she'd flopped to the floor, preoccupied with readjusting her body's response to another overdose of morphine. Anja's own bio-readings predicted shock, and she began to shiver. The elevator platform came to a rest, and she staggered for it.

A hand grabbed the back of her neck and Anja's ocular mapping measured her forehead's impact with the platform's edge in nanoseconds.

Her ocular interface flashed white, red, and then returned to blue, spinning damage assessments. A forehead gash; a concussion. Warnings flashed of energy reserves draining for self-repair protocols. Aine-7 grabbed her shoulder and flipped her over.

Anja coughed shining blood that lifted into the air. She'd

bitten her own tongue.

"Look at you, blinking and flashing like a child's toy. Warning. Waaarning," Aine lightly singsonged. She took hold of Anja's chin.

"Sixth, watch me. Watch me." The lights at Aine-7's temple glowed. "This is the blessed circlet of a Perfect."

Pure ice-lights blinded, and the warning flashes washed to white before Anja's eyes.

Aine the Fourth, she thought, coming for dying warriors.

Aine-7 lifted Anja's chin and turned her face, studying it.

"Your nose is still bleeding," she softly reproached, letting go. "Oh, Sixth. You're no executioner. But I realized something when you came here." Aine's hands smoothed down Anja's body, searching. "Perhaps I woke up in this ugly, forgotten place...." She pressed lips to Anja's forehead. "To be yours. That thought occurred to Aine the Second when Aine the Third came for her."

"Our—memories—" Her right arm's stump moved uselessly to halt Aine-7's wandering hands. She swallowed blood. "Our memories are locked by the gods." Where was Kyn? She needed to delay. "We—we recall nothing before Aine the Fourth."

"True...but I was not made by gods." Aine pressed close, smelling of leather and Kyn. She smiled, seemingly fond. "I remember your life."

Anja's breath halted, her thoughts wild and jumbled. An explosion suddenly sounded, and the ceiling trembled.

"The lab's destruction." Aine's tone was pleased. "I've a surprise too. I made a little something while you had me locked out. The fleshmorphs *can* self-repair—when someone helps them."

Anja gripped Aine-7 by her dress's front.

"Now Sixth." She caressed the back of Anja's hand. "Don't you want to hear about the timer I placed on the entrance? It should open the lab doors right…now."

Ben's high-pitched scream echoed above.

Aine-7 kissed Anja's bloody mouth.

"I'll take good care of her," she whispered solemnly. She snatched the fountain pen from Anja's breast pocket.

The steel nib descended for Anja's right eye and pierced the ocular interface, shattering it.

Anja lay, limbs splayed.

Aine-7 gently pulled the pen out, the barrel squelching from Anja's eye socket, and globules of shining blood detached and drifted up.

Wiping the gore away, she read the inscription: *The stars, your gift, Aine the Sixth.*

She slipped the pen into the leather jacket's inner pocket and patted it: a souvenir.

An explosion sounded—the room tilted for a second, and Aine frowned, realizing that it was herself tilting and not the room. She wiped at the perspiration on her forehead, leaving a shining smear.

When she rose with Anja in her arms, her knees buckled. Black dots danced before her ocular interface and the world spun.

Another blast boomed nearer, and Aine grinned. Anja loved chain reactions. The end-blast was certain to be in the bio-waste room.

Equilibrium parameters readjusting, she wrapped an arm around Anja and dragged herself to the matter recycler's glowing maw. Convulsions overtook her body when they reached the threshold, and she hugged Anja to steady herself.

Anja's bloodied face smudged the leather. A shining drop lifted from Anja's cheek to ascend into the air. Aine caressed the still face, lit by the whirling light of the recycler.

"Vahalla," she softly said.

Kyn snarled, hackles on end, and her back cracked as her spine lengthened more.

A mountainous lump of dismembered Femflesh squeezed through the lab entrance. Squirming arm and leg parts interweaved from a central mass of heads and torsos to form four giant limbs. Lips and orifices smacked. An elephantine appendage rose, its hands and hoof bits wiggling, and a stench of decay issued, making Kyn nearly retch. Ben slipped and fell down before the monster.

Kyn sprang for him and swept him aside. The limb came down and slammed her to the ground, smothering her with the dead weight and stickiness of rotting flesh. The creature left her like a smear on the floor and plodded for Ben.

"Ann," Ben yelled, clambering. "*Ann.*" He coughed as smoke from the burning transformer enveloped.

Kyn unstuck herself from the floor. Through the haze and beyond Ben, emergency lights flashed—the rejuvenator near the decontamination shower. A high-pitched whine issued—

Anja—of course, she thought.

Kyn's muscles enlarged, splitting her tee shirt. Her jaw cracked and stretched, and a snout full of teeth erupted. When the flesh monster brought a squirming limb down for

Ben, Kyn leapt with a silent howl.

She caught the limb with claws digging and whipped her body around. The creature tripped over Ben and fell for the overheating juice station. An appendage caught in the bed, and Kyn hopped over the undulating mass of fused heads and torsos to slam the glass lid. Cables loudly popped in a rain of sparks as she bounded away, and white plumes of fumes ejected. Kyn grabbed Ben and tossed him behind the decontamination shower.

The rejuvenator's detonation deafened and flattened Kyn to the floor. Glass and burning flesh rained, and she smelled the blow coming for her back before she felt it.

WHUMP

The strike caught her shoulder as she rolled aside, her leg whipping up to kick the mass of limbs away. Loping across the floor on all fours, she grabbed a cowering Ben by the scruff. She spied something—

Through the smoke and showers of sparks, a second rejuvenator ahead blinked its emergency lights. The familiar whine began. Taking to her feet, she bowled Ben past the overloading unit. He skidded across the lab and past a third juice station that also flashed red. When he tumbled to a stop near his office, he groaned. She hoped he got the hint and used the stairs—

WHAM

The blow sent Kyn flying off her feet and impacting the shower, shattering the glass. She landed in a heap on the other side and next to the second rejuvenator that smoked. Her bleary gaze took in the lumbering mountain of flesh and its remaining three appendages struggling to reach her.

One limb shot for her. Sparks showered her back as she caught the mass of wiggling flesh and pulled the creature in.

It tipped into the rejuvenator's bed. She scrambled out from between its bracing limbs.

The ear-splitting boom nearly knocked Kyn onto her face. The creature's top half blew apart, flaming body parts smacking Kyn as she galloped away on all fours. Weighted flesh then struck the floor—again—then again—the creature's remaining mass cartwheeling in pursuit. Ben ran out of his office and hastily pocketed something. He took one look at Kyn and sped down the stairs.

Kyn dashed past the third rejuvenator as it spewed fumes. She leapt the stairwell right when the juice station combusted.

She landed on the floor, seeing flames fly but no bits of fleshmorph. Above, the flesh creature teetered in flames, a blob joining two remaining limbs. It plummeted over the railing for Kyn.

It hit the ground, multitudinous fingers and hooves scrabbling. Kyn leapt the dented steel table with the burning creature slithering after. It pulled itself over the tabletop, smoke billowing and flames licking, and Kyn sunk claws into its body.

With a silent roar, she hauled the beast up and slammed its wriggling mass inside the materializer.

Blackened hands and legs reached for her. Mouths sucked against the materializer's glass and breasts squished. Kyn tried to shove the cover shut and it jammed on a ropey heap of woven limbs, still on fire. The writhing appendage grabbed the cover and pushed back.

Kyn's feet skidded on the floor as she held on, and she realized: maybe Anja never got around to tampering with the materializer.

The machine suddenly hummed, and its interior lit, energy

beams pounding. The bulk of flesh shuddered like milk in a mixer, and the cover rattled in Kyn's hands. She abandoned it and bounded away.

When she glanced back, the entire machine shook from the thumping of bombarded body parts, and the smell of cooked, spoiled meat hit the smoke-filled air. The weave of limbs lifted and erupted into flames.

SPLAT.

Liquefied flesh painted the materializer's insides. The machine grew still and its lights died. Rendered synth-pulp bubbled up and oozed to the floor. Kyn swiveled: did Anja return from below to activate the machine?

Only Ben met her scrutiny, his hands at a workstation. He slumped. Kyn ran for the missing elevator platform and jumped into the red-lit pit below.

Kyn landed, smelling the blood of a Perfect.

In a room lit red and with flesh-waste surrounding them, Aine sat by the recycler's open mouth, its interior light haloing her shining hair. She cradled a still Anja in her arms.

Aine-7's head snapped up as if she'd nodded off, and she stared, disorientated.

Anja?

Kyn stepped, ashen.

Aine looked down.

"I got your jacket dirty," she said, embarrassed.

The burned off limb; the injured eye. Her face. Anja's lights had died, and Kyn could not tell if Anja breathed.

A silent whine began in her throat. She would howl. She diminished in size, bones cracking and her snout receding.

When her transformation ended, only the woman stood, and Kyn held back the lamenting hound within that would bay.

"Kyn." Perspiration beaded on Aine's forehead, and her pupils filled her irises. "I only did what they wanted you to do. Because I'm Seventh, Kyn. I am here now, and I am Seventh.

"You feared her secret future. You feared your role in it. But myself...what was I made for? Look at me, Kyn.

"Surely I am more," she said earnestly. "If I am the Aine who may walk the universe—free—won't I change the fate of the Aines?" Her hand went to her heart. "Won't I finally transcend the old purpose? Unlike Sixth, I'm yours."

Kyn's hand opened by her side. She wanted Anja.

Aine beamed, brilliant. She rose, and Anja slipped from her lap. Aine-7's limbs jerked when she stood. She moved for Kyn and pressed close. Her lips met Kyn's mouth.

When she pulled back, her smile faded.

"Kyn," she said.

Kyn stared at the blood smear on Aine-7's unwounded brow.

"Do you think I'm a mistake, Kyn?" Aine whispered.

Her smile returned, tremulous. "Or a threat?"

My time comes, Aine the Fourth said.

Aine raised her bloodstained hand as if she would cup Kyn's face. Tremors wracked the limb. She brought the trembling fingers back and touched her own cheek and the tear that fell there.

"If I had been an ordinary woman, you'd have forgiven." Her eyes brimmed, glimmering. "You're so beautiful."

She stepped back, wobbly, and grinned.

'It's okay, Kyn," she said, hushed.

It's okay, Kyn, Aine-5 said.

Kyn touched her own eyes.

Close your eyes, she said.

Aine's eyes were distant and shining.

She closed her eyes.

Kyn struck, her knife-hand cleaving flesh and cranium.

Kyn was weeping.

Repairing.

Anja's undamaged eye's interface flashed behind her eyelid.

Beneath the roar of the matter recycler, desperate breath issued. It was the breath only the silent could sob. A sound known to her, heard when Aine the Fourth's eyes dimmed forever.

I am not dead, she wanted to say.

Instead, her mouth attempted to say: *Kyn, recycler overload imminent.*

Anja's eye opened.

Shining blood ascended. Globules drifted up from a limp body Kyn cradled, dressed in her leather jacket. Before the bright, open mouth of the recycler, Kyn stood rooted, as if the body she held could still cling, resisting entry into the maw.

Anja's hand scrambled for purchase on the floor. She flung herself and collided with Kyn.

"Leave—her," she uttered. Her own grip dragged Aine's body down. "Recycler overload imminent."

In the Pong, a manhole cover disengaged and flipped, the

top thumping on the street. Kyn emerged from the man-hole to a sparkling night, and Anja clung to Kyn's back and looked up, her one eye blinking.

The habitat sectors' lights twinkled above, the patterns marred by smoke plumes. In the Pong, the Femflesh build-ing burned.

Ben crawled out of the hole and pulled off his emergen-cy lab mask. Dropping it, he staggered away and down the street. Anja raised her missing arm to halt him. She realized belatedly: what if he'd backed up what she'd destroyed?

Mustering words, she coughed instead. Kyn swung Anja around and into a cradle carry. The twinkling darkness spun, and Anja swallowed, dizzy. Ben disappeared into the night with Kyn hardly noticing.

Her crushing embrace barely allowed Anja breath. Kyn dropped on to a crate behind a neon-lit noodle cart and hud-dled, Anja tight against her.

Kyn's stark and distant gaze took in the mix of possible concern and guarded curiosity from the noodle cart owner and his sole patron and dismissed it. She might accept kind-ness, but preferred the two stay where they were. Something niggled in her numbed mind, needing attention.

An arm stump wrapped in a tourniquet made from her torn shirt prodded her in the chin.

"Kyn?" Anja murmured. The blood crusting her shut eye shone.

The last remnant of Kyn's tee hung from one of her arms. She pulled it off and then gently wiped Anja's nose and mouth with the cloth.

Gratitude; shouldn't Kyn feel that? With Anja breathing still, able to speak and think still? But the scent of fresh, Perfect blood hollowed out her soul and resurrected the memory of another place, another death.

And the memory of Aine-7.

A fire suppression truck approached, lights and horns blaring. Kyn turned to block Anja with her body and pressed her head close as if they might be kissing, and the vehicle sped by. The team would flush the Femflesh building and shortly, Skycourt operatives might appear. She needed to take Anja away.

"Kyn," Anja whispered.

Kyn's breath hitched. Anja's voice, Aine's voice…her shining blood blooming and lifting from Kyn's hand. That's what she forgot to do. Cleanse her hand.

Anja gripped the bloodstained fingers Kyn raised before her own face.

"It's okay, Kyn."

Kyn fiercely blinked.

Her tears fell to the memory of diamond drops ascending, and Nuit Four rotated.

Next: *Predacious*

PREVIEW: MONSTER STALKER

Kill first.

CHAPTER ONE :

NOW ARRIVING

NICO was a bullet, piercing matter. She burst into dusky skies, an airfield fast approaching her face. She hit it and rolled.

Sun! Clouds shrouded it, but she felt its heat. She scrambled on the tarmac and saw no earth to bury herself in. When she didn't catch fire, she touched the black surface she knelt on, warmed by sunlight. Her free hand clutched her switchblade, its blade triggered. The hot handle sparked with electricity.

"Ow—ow," Nico said. She dropped her blade, pulled down her cardigan's sleeve over her burnt palm, then picked the knife up again.

Airfield? Buildings stood on the hazy horizon. She needed to run for cover. When she tried to stand, she plopped back instead. The airfield tilted as she fought nausea.

Mr. Bear, her sandy-coloured stuffed bear, sat strapped to the front of her black cardigan and white button-down. Nico looked down at the chest harness, made of leather, silver grommets, and fastenings, and could not remember purchasing it, much less donning it. Her left knee throbbed, and she raised it to look.

Beneath her short black skirt with the two pleats, her black stocking had torn at the knee; the bloodied bruise already healing from where she'd scraped it on landing. She had no memory of choosing her clothes or her shoes (which were the spike-studded leather oxfords and not her black Mary Janes) though it was an outfit she wore often.

A man in uniform coveralls and a ball cap with the logo *Jifk* walked across the airfield towards her. Somehow, she'd missed his approach. His tattooed face appeared friendly, and Nico thought his markings looked Maori. An identification badge dangled from his breast pocket: *Tane.*

Nico blinked. She'd read that in Cyrillic, but then it rearranged itself into the Latin alphabet.

"Here's another one," he said to no one in particular, though Nico couldn't be certain he spoke to someone via a mic. "Hey there. Can you put that away, please?" Nico looked at her blade, then shut it. "Thanks. Welcome to Again NewYork. I'm going to ask you to step over here and stand in that circle, and we'll get you processed right away." He brought up a rectangular-shaped device in his hand. "What's your name?"

"A—Again, New York?" Nico said.

"No, really. That's your name?" He indicated again that she move towards a circle blacker than the tarmac it lay in. She hadn't noticed it during her scrambling.

Nico tucked her switchblade into her skirt's waistband in back and rose. She stumbled to her feet, woozy. "No, I'm Nico," she said. "Nicolette Alexikova." Adrenaline receding, she felt a little like she'd been struck by lightning; her hair rose from static electricity. She looked at the pitch-black circle that resembled a pit, then at Tane. "Why am I—am I going to—?"

"Nope. You won't." Tane answered. Nico toed the blackness; it felt solid. "Both feet, please," Tane added. She put both feet into the circle.

Everything flashed, and she threw up her arms. When she looked down at herself and Bear, they were still in one piece.

"Vampire, right?" Tane touched his pad.

Nico froze.

"Well, your bio-dats say you are," Tane said. "And boy, did you get skittish when you saw you were in daylight."

Nico gave her surroundings a furtive look. "Again...New York?"

"Right." Tane continued to enter data. "Your teddy bear doesn't appear to be alive or sentient, so that's just one to process for immigration. Can you confirm that you're a vampire, please?"

"Yes. Yes I am," she said bravely. "And I've dual citizenship—American and British."

Tane looked up and grinned. "If that matters to you. But on Darqueworld, designations like that don't exist; the city-states are only what the gods make of them."

Darkworld? Nico tried to look closer at his badge. Electricity buzzed along her skin, and the air exploded, popping her ears. She ducked and looked behind her. Farther down the field, the atmosphere split. It erupted in fire and ejected a flaming man, the ends of his trench coat trailing. He tumbled on the ground and flopped to a stop. The hole sucked in upon itself and disappeared.

"Wow, what an entry—right out of an explosion." Tane's tone was matter-of-fact. Two bulky men blipped into view, and Nico blinked, thinking they'd stepped on to the tarmac as if from an invisible place. The men ran up to the one smoking on the ground—at least, Nico thought the two were men. Like Tane, they wore coveralls, but horns grew out of their heads, and their features had snouts and brows like bulls. Nico turned to Tane.

"Am I in purgatory?" she said.

Tane scrutinised her. "Don't know how you got here, huh? Memory loss." He entered something into his pad. "Don't worry, they'll have a Po get a good look at you, then assign you a social worker—"

"Social worker? *Now* I believe in hell."

"Oh, is that what you think this is?" Tane's tone was light.

"No...hell is getting murdered and stuff." Nico tried to ignore the sound of the two horned guys scraping the smoking fellow off the ground.

"It sure is. Hey," he said, catching her attention. "You're a chrono-immigrant, if that info helps—" He pointed at his head. "Jog your memory some. You took a trip to a planet settled by others like yourself, and here you are. I only need you to tell me your era. I'm betting it's late twentieth century."

Nico looked at him blankly. "The year is 1998."

"Great. Now, if you'll show me the back of your hand." He pulled out a device resembling a tattoo gun.

"What's that?" she said, wary.

"A biometric tagger." Tane motioned for her hand. Nico presented the back of her left hand, wondering if she was about to receive a barcode tattoo. Tane placed the tagger over her skin. A beam burst, pricking her. It felt like an inoculation. Then she remembered that as a vampire, she had no fear of diseases. The sensation ran up her wrist after Tane lifted the tagger, and she shook her hand, trying to rid herself of the tickle.

If I'm in a coma somewhere, someone just did something funny to my hand.

She wasn't certain if vampires could fall into actual comas, and dismissed that speculation. Tane gestured to a metal arch that Nico hadn't noticed before.

"All done! Enter that gate there, and you'll be processed and ready to start your new life in Again NewYork."

★

Chrono-immigrant? Nico approached the gate. It showed only the airfield beyond it. If everything happening was her conscious reality, perhaps the forethought of strapping Mr Bear to herself made sense. But what situation had she come out of, especially with blade drawn? Nico looked down in case she'd missed signs of violence on her person or clothes. She did not seek fights, but evil could follow a girl, as she well knew. If she'd been in danger in Leningrad before coming to...Again, New York, she couldn't recall what had happened or why.

Therefore, I was kidnapped somehow, and now I'm in some rich man's fantasy set. Or this is some crazy KGB plot to get vampires to out themselves.

She stepped through the gate.

And found herself in a security area aglow in dim blue, one with bored officers standing by roped-off stations and machines. None of the officers looked human, though humanoid enough. A great, glass bubble hung in the room's centre; inside a large, bald female head floated. She looked at Nico.

I'll ignore that. Nico stared instead at a pedestal sign with an illustration of a bald person's head in a bubble, accompanied by possibly important information. Nico couldn't read the language, so she returned her attention to the room.

A quick scan (while avoiding the staring head) seemed to affirm that she was the lone chrono-immigrant present. She hoped no one would confiscate her switchblade—Tane had not seemed to mind her carrying it. Nico checked her hand, not wanting an injury to delay processing. Thanks to a vampire's healing ability, the burn was gone and her skin, whole. She approached the nearest station, where a blue humanoid male looked down at her, impassive On the counter sat a mounted tagger like the one Tane had used, and a large metal orb with a glass top. The blue male held up a lens.

The lens flashed, making Nico see colours, and the back of her hand itched.

"*Raqa,*" he said, indicating the mounted tagger.

"You want my hand, right?" Nico said, and then noticed what the orb contained. An insect as large as a rat sat within, wearing a tiny badge. It waved feelers and seemed to look at her with its multi-faceted eyes.

"*Click-click*," it said, its mandibles moving. Nico thrust her hand beneath the tagger, suppressing the urge to wallop the bug and run away. Rising in a shallow forest grave with beetles living in her mouth had not endeared her to insects. The bug pressed something on its tiny console.

The beam that hit her hand seared, but Nico saw no burn on her skin. She shook her hand again.

"Read that, please," the insect said motioning to its glass hatch, and Nico started in surprise. She was certain it had made more clicking sounds. A message illuminated across the orb's glass. Hieroglyphics rearranged, forming the Latin alphabet.

"*Hi farhol mal haro sowo*," she read, bewildered. The insect's mouth clicked more, and the blue humanoid appeared to guffaw, as if they were sharing a laugh. Nico gave them a look, hoping they hadn't made her say something obscene.

"Translate for us, please," the insect requested, and somehow the translation came to Nico.

"My hovercraft is full of...eels," Nico said sourly. *That's it. This is a dream.* She enjoyed Monty Python well enough, but not that much. The blue humanoid and the insect chortled more.

"Translation tag functioning. Step that way, please," the insect said.

★

Officers waved her off two more stations after they flashed lenses at her. Nico was glad; their stations looked like medical facilities. At the second one, a man in a double-breasted pinstripe suit, wingtips, and askew fedora lay inert on the dais, having succumbed to whatever procedure he'd received. Two bald humanoids in smocks held pads and discussed data over him. Nico hurried to the last station, where a black circle lay, similar to the one in the airfield. The bored female officer standing before it gestured in its direction. She laid a three-fingered hand on Nico's shoulder to guide her.

"Don't touch me," Nico said automatically. "Um, sorry."

Nico stepped into the circle. When it flashed, Nico felt as if her underwear had been frisked.

"Hey! Mr Bear! My stuff!" she exclaimed, seeing her possessions lying in a neat row on the table, and hurried off the circle to fetch Bear.

"Can you tell us where Mr Bear comes from, please," the officer said in a bored tone, seating herself before a monitor.

"Mr Bear comes from where I came from," Nico said. "He's —"

Her thought slid away on a white surface in her mind.

"He's..." Nico frowned.

The officer glanced at something above Nico's shoulder, and when she turned to look, the floating head was staring in her direction. Nico turned back again.

"Okay, thank you," the officer said, dismissive, and Nico assumed the questioning was done.

While Nico placed Bear in his harness again, a nude man, completely hairless to his non-existent eyebrows, walked by, bypassing the search area. In his two hands he held a claymore over four feet long, the blade pointing down. Nico looked at the giant blade and then at him.

This is the most Freudian dream ever.

He moved ahead as she picked up her switchblade and put it back in her waistband. Before she pocketed her Chococat wallet, she opened it. It contained rubles, her Leningrad University student ID, a credit card, a Leningrad metro pass, and her magazine clipping of the actress Sabella Peck, dressed in a men's suit. Nico hugged the picture to her and Bear, then put her wallet away. Her passport security neck wallet had also ended up on the table; she grabbed it and the tin of breath mints she hadn't known she'd been carrying. When she glanced back at the room, wondering if it was okay to leave, the female head in the bubble coolly watched her. Nico walked quickly to where the naked man had exited.

"It's
vampires,
all the way
down."

A DARQUEPUNK
NOVEL

BLOODY
NIKE

ELIZABETH WATASIN

More from Elizabeth:

The Dark Victorian: Risen Vol 1
The Dark Victorian: Bones Vol 2
Ice Demon: A Dark Victorian Penny Dread Vol 1
Medusa: A Dark Victorian Penny Dread Vol 2
Sundark: An Elle Black Penny Dread Vol 1
Poison Garden: An Elle Black Penny Dread Vol 2
Monster Stalker: A Darquepunk Novel Vol 1
Bloody Nike: A Darquepunk Novel Vol 2
Charm School Graphique Vol 1
and
Charm School Digital No 1-9

The Wrecking Faerie: A Charm School Novella Vol 1
Hot Roddin' To Hell: A Charm School Novella Vol 2

About The Author

Elizabeth Watasin is the author of the Gothic steampunk series *The Dark Victorian*, The *Elle Black Penny Dreads*, the *Darquepunk* series, and the creator/artist of the indie comics series *Charm School*. She is the winner of the 2015 Rainbow Award for Best Lesbian Fantasy and Romance Fantasy and a Gaylactic Spectrum nominee. A twenty year veteran of animation and comics, her credits include thirteen feature films, such as *Beauty and the Beast*, *Aladdin*, *The Lion King*, and *The Princess and the Frog*, and writing for *Disney Adventures* magazine. She lives in Los Angeles with her black cat named Draw, bringing readers uncanny heroines in cyberpunk, historical fantasy, diesal fantasy, and paranormal thrillers.

Sign up for the mailing list at A-Girl Studio.
www.a-girlstudio.com
amazon.com/author/elizabethwatasin
www.facebook.com/ElizabethWatasinX
twitter.com/ewatasin

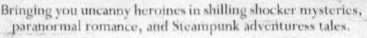

ELIZABETH WATASIN

The DARK
VICTORIAN

BONES